Kah Wilde

THE STONEHEART BRIDE

Flora doesn't know which is worse: being abducted by ogres who intend to eat her, or being saved by the barbarian warrior who'd coldly rejected her hand in marriage. Brom the Stonehearted had crushed Flora's every hope of a future where she was valued for herself, and dreams of a life where she was more than her uncle's political pawn.

But as they ride toward home, Flora discovers that a warrior raised in the barren wilds of the Dead Lands recognizes value far beyond power and gold—and that his particular kind of courtship could never be cold…

PRETTY BRIDE

As keeper of a sacred oath, Aruk allows nothing to tempt him away from his duty. Not gold, not women, not power. So when the barbarian warrior is marooned in the middle of the ocean, his only thought is of escaping the island paradise and continuing his quest.

Until a pretty princess washes up onto the beach. Spoiled and disobedient, Jalisa should have been easy to resist. But when Aruk discovers the secrets concealed by her beautiful smile, he'll have to decide between his duty and his heart…

THE MIDNIGHT BRIDE

To save her family from a tyrant king, Mara of Aremond must win a tournament—and she won't let anyone stop her from claiming the prize. Especially not Strax, the barbarian warrior who has tormented her every step of the way. But when a sorcerer's trap binds them together, Mara must decide whether Strax is her greatest enemy, or if everything she seeks can only be found in the barbarian's arms…

THREE
DEAD LAND
BRIDES
KATI WILDE

Also by Kati Wilde

The Hellfire Riders MC Romance
(Discreet Cover Editions)

SAXON

BLOWBACK

GUNNER

BULL & DUKE

STONE

(Original Covers & Ebooks)

THE HELLFIRE RIDERS: SAXON & JENNY

THE HELLFIRE RIDERS: JACK & LILY

BREAKING IT ALL

GIVING IT ALL

CRAVING IT ALL

FAKING IT ALL

LOSING IT ALL

Contemporary Holiday Romances
(Discreet Cover Editions)

SECRET SANTA & ALL HE WANTS FOR CHRISTMAS

THE WEDDING NIGHT BEFORE CHRISTMAS

(Original Covers & Ebooks)

SECRET SANTA

ALL HE WANTS FOR CHRISTMAS

THE WEDDING NIGHT

The Dead Lands

(Discreet Cover Editions)

The Midwinter Bride

Three Dead Land Brides

(Original Covers & Ebooks)

The Midwinter Mail-Order Bride

The Midnight Bride

Pretty Bride

The Stoneheart Bride

The Midsummer Bride

(coming soon)

Wolfkin & Berserkers

Beauty In Spring

High Moon

Teacher's Pet Wolf

Sheriff's Bad Bear

(coming soon)

Contemporary Romance

Going Nowhere Fast[1]

The King's Horrible Bride

Fantasy Romance

Evil Twin[2]

---

[1] Includes cameos by the Hellfire Riders

[2] Set in the same world as the Dead Lands

Contents

The StoneHeart Bride

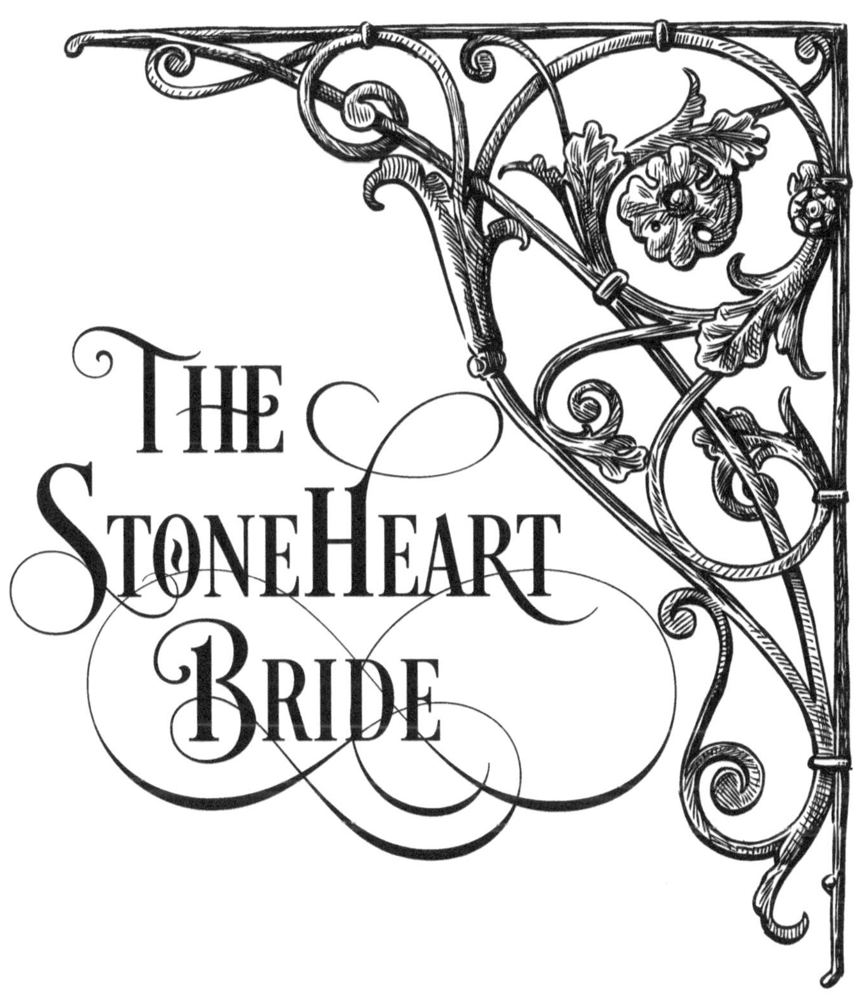

A DEAD LANDS FANTASY ROMANCE

OGRE MOUNTAINS
THE DEAD LANDS
STONEHEART TERRITORY
HUNTING GROUNDS
THE KINGDOM OF INNIS
THE STONEHEART BRIDE
N
W E
S
Not to scale. Physical features and distances are exaggerated for clarity and fun.
© KATI WILDE

ERE WE ARE, AT THE BEGINNING OF THREE TALES OF BRIDES driven by both hope and fear, and who find happiness in the arms of barbarians who hail from a land long ago sundered by a magical Reckoning.

First comes the stonehearted warrior.

The time is anotherwhen, a date unknown but in the midst of summer; the place is anotherwhere, a world unnamed but far east of the Illwind Sea. And this story begins, as many stories do, with a woman whose heart was broken by careless words, but whose strength and determination will never fail.

So we settle in for a short spell—for that is all a tale is, words woven together in hopes of making magic. It matters not if you believe in such things. You must only believe this—

Love is magic, too.

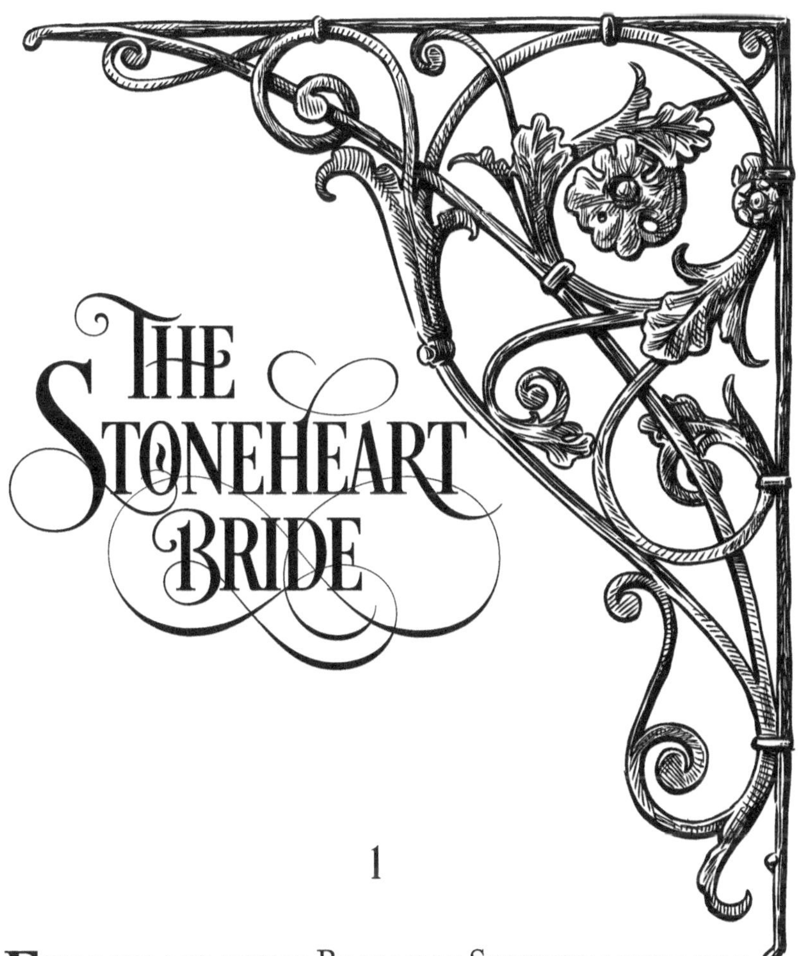

THE STONEHEART BRIDE

1

Five days ago, when Brom the Stonehearted had rejected Flora's hand in marriage, the agony that had ripped through her chest made her wonder if a broken heart was truly shredded from within. But five days ago, Flora hadn't guessed that she would soon know the answer.

Well, *she* wouldn't know it, because she would be dead. But the two ogres who'd abducted Flora would see whether her heart was literally a broken mess when they tore her body apart and devoured her flesh.

Which would likely happen as soon as they finished arguing over who got the juiciest bits.

"I claim her plump haunch," one of the hideous giants declared, while smacking his slimy lips and tossing an armload of fallen boughs onto their fire.

The other scoffed as he used his monstrous stone axe to hack at the tree limb that would become Flora's roasting spit. "What of it? She has two haunches. I'll take the second."

"Have you forgotten our purpose, fool?" the first ogre spat through jagged teeth. "Upon the left haunch is the birthmark that will prove who she was to those who find the remains."

"Then leave her head and the ring with the royal crest. They will know the jewel and her face."

"Our orders are to also leave the marked haunch."

"We could say that we did leave it, but that an animal of the forest must have carried it off," said the second ogre with a sly, wet grin.

Lying on her side at the edge of the small clearing, Flora tried not to listen. Truly she did. She was already terrified, and further panic wouldn't help her escape during the short time that the ogres were preoccupied with building the fire. The horror of the day had already taken its toll—first when the guards in her hunting party had been slaughtered, then when she'd been bound, gagged, and tossed over the back of her horse, followed by endless hours of travel to the border of her uncle's kingdom. If she succumbed to her fear now, she'd never free herself from the ropes binding her hands and feet.

Yet until Flora heard the ogres speaking, she'd thought they'd only taken her along as a snack. She hadn't realized they had a more heinous purpose.

They meant to start a war. And their actions today *would* start it. When Flora's uncle discovered her remains, he'd march his army into the mountainous territory held by the ogre overlord…where her uncle might eventually be victorious, but not before thousands of his soldiers were killed in those battles.

Flora could *not* let her life be the cause of so much death.

Steely resolve steadied her trembling fingers, and Flora blindly searched the ground behind her bound hands for a sharp stone or a pointed stick—anything that she might use to free herself.

Nothing but dirt and leaves.

Panic began to take hold again when the ogres finished their preparations at the roasting fire. Flora's heart stuttered as they turned in her direction. Their greedy eyes roamed hungrily over her nude form, and terror wormed through her muscles like a parasite, leeching her strength…but not her resolve. Frantically she squirmed backward through the dirt, not giving up—though the brutes laughed at her futile attempts to get away.

"Even if your feet were free, human, you could never outrun us." The first ogre started toward her, unsheathing the blade that, earlier in the day, had butchered Flora's guards. "But fear will season your meat, so a chase would make our feast all the more deli—"

Abruptly he stopped—mid-word, mid-step, mid-*thunk*—though Flora in her desperation to escape hardly knew whence that heavy, fleshy *thunk* had come.

That is, until the ogre collapsed onto the ground with an axe protruding from the back of his skull.

Shock held her immobile for the briefest moment. Had the second ogre betrayed the first, so that he could gorge on her meat without sharing even a haunch? But when her gaze darted to him, the ogre still standing did not look toward Flora at all. Instead he held his giant axe at ready as his foul gaze searched the utter dark of the nighttime forest.

All seemed quiet, but for the crackling of the flames and the thundering of her heart.

Until the ogre shouted, "Face me! So I might pick her flesh from my teeth with your splintered bones!"

On the far side of the clearing, a solid shadow emerged from the trees. The bulk of the ogre's body and the glare of the fire blocked Flora's view, and she had only the impression of hardened muscle and a gleaming broadsword before the ogre charged. The strike of stone against steel rang a fast and furious peal, underscored by deep grunts and the ogre's furious roar. For an instant, Flora watched the battle with her heart lifting and lifting, buoyed by the hope that her rescue had come—then sheer dread lodged sickeningly in her throat as she realized that whatever had slaughtered the first ogre might be *worse* than they were.

Wildly she fought against her bindings, but her struggles only dislodged the cord wound around her head. She spit the gag from her dry mouth. Her heaving breaths came harsh and loud, her world narrowing to the bite of rope into her skin, the slickness at her wrists that must be blood but she didn't stop fighting, praying the blood would lubricate her bindings enough to wrest her hands free.

Then awareness seeped in.

All was quiet again.

The ogre was dead. A small whimper escaped Flora's throat when she spotted the giant's bloodied body—and his head, the severed neck dripping gore, as it was tossed aside with a flick of the other combatant's wrist. *A human,* Flora saw and gave a sudden sob of relief.

But her relief only lasted until the warrior turned toward her, and the fire cast flickering orange light over his face. A face she knew too well.

Brom the Stonehearted.

Fresh agony split open her heart, a pain made all the worse because of the joy that came with it—the joy that Flora couldn't help but feel every time she saw him, the joy that had accompanied her nearly every moment that she'd spent with Brom over the past two months. Flora's uncle had wanted to form an alliance with the barbarians that had settled in the wilderness east of the Kingdom of Innis, and so her cousin, Prince Vash, had made the initial foray into that territory. Once there, Vash had befriended the leader of the Stoneheart Clan, then persuaded Brom and a dozen of his warriors to travel to Innis and begin negotiations with the king—and the day of Brom's arrival marked the day that Flora made the most devastating mistake of her life.

She'd begun to hope.

It had been by King Martas's order that Flora had served as Brom's guide and companion whenever Prince Vash was unavailable—a command that had initially terrified her. She'd known that her uncle intended to one day marry her off to cement a political alliance, and that he wouldn't care what sort of man her husband would be. Wouldn't care if he was cruel or cold, faithless or weak. As long as Flora's marriage could strengthen his own position, King Martas would force her to wed. So it was with dread that she'd met the barbarian warrior her cousin brought home.

Yet instead of cruel or weak, Brom proved honorable and strong. And—complete and utter fool that she was—Flora had begun to dream of a future where she might be wanted and valued by her husband. Perhaps even cherished by him.

Never before had she dared dream of such happiness. Yet each hour she'd spent with Brom had given her courage. Each time he'd sought her company on her daily hunts. Each time he'd chosen the seat next to her at the king's table. Each time she'd made him grin, or when she'd teased out his deep and rumbling laugh. Each time his dark gaze had settled on her lips, and his big body seemed filled with the same hot tension that kept Flora's senses in a constant, burning grip. And in the recent weeks, as their conversations had deepened and she'd revealed more of her private thoughts to him, the looks he'd given had appeared almost…tender. As if he might have begun to care for her. As if he might have even begun to cherish her. At least a little.

So five days ago, when her uncle informed Flora that he intended to offer her hand to Brom and negotiate her bride price, pure joy had engulfed her heart. With giddy anticipation, she'd waited outside the chamber where King Martas and his councilors sat with Brom and his warriors, hammering out the details of an alliance. She'd trembled with happiness as her uncle proposed a marriage between Brom and Flora in order to solidify the new ties between their people.

Brom had immediately and coldly refused.

But she hadn't lost hope then. Flora knew how such negotiations worked. Brom must want something *more* from her uncle…and her uncle, who was convinced that an alliance with Stoneheart's warriors was the kingdom's only chance of defending against a rumored attack by the ogres from the north, was willing to give more. Yet gold, horses, and steel were all refused, and each rejection shredded a little of Flora's hope.

Then her uncle had cried out in frustration, "What can I give that you would take my niece to wed?"

Each word of Brom's reply had been ruthless and sharp, like icy blades piercing her chest. "*Never* could you make an offer for her hand that I would accept."

Heart utterly destroyed, Flora had fled.

Only sheer willpower had gotten her through the following days. Willpower, along with a determined effort to avoid him. It had taken all of Flora's strength to keep from bursting into tears whenever Brom was near. So she'd stayed away when she could—and when she could not, she'd survived by clinging to the tattered remnants of her pride. No more did she reveal any of herself in conversations; instead she spoke as little as possible before escaping his presence…and never did she glance at him. Not when she might see the same look in his eyes that she'd mistaken so badly before, that warm and tender expression that had made Flora believe he wanted her and cherished her.

Such a fool she'd been.

Yet now, *now*—Brom was *here*. And he'd broken her heart…but then he'd saved her. With hot tears clogging her throat, Flora watched as he stepped over the ogre's body and strode across the clearing, his broad chest glistening with sweat and blood—every inch a barbarian warrior, fierce and strong and utterly magnificent.

While she lay tied and naked and helpless, with the remaining shreds of her pride scattered like trash in the dirt.

Humiliation and relief collided violently within her chest, ripping free a harsh sob. Brom's stride faltered, then he crouched at her side. His massive fists clenched, knuckles whitening under smears of blood, and even without looking up Flora knew that he was cataloguing each bruise on her flesh, each scrape of her skin. Each injury must make him furious, because even though he didn't want to marry her, even though he didn't care for her as she'd dreamed, Brom the Stonehearted was still a good man—and rage was a good man's response to seeing *anyone* treated as she'd been.

But at least she couldn't mistake anger for a softer emotion and fool herself again. Shaking, Flora lifted her gaze to his face. The fury she expected to see burned in the shadows of his eyes and the taut line of his mouth— yet as his gaze met hers, as his big hand opened as if to cradle her cheek, she saw the same tenderness that she'd been so wrong about before.

Renewed misery ravaged her heart. "Don't touch me!" she cried out, cringing away from his reach.

Brom froze. And it must have been only a trick of the flickering flames and the blur of her tears that made her imagine the anguish that swept across his expression. A blink later, his face seemed carved from stone.

His throat worked before he said, "Are you badly hurt?"

His voice had a thick and ragged edge that she'd never heard before, yet she couldn't pause to consider the meaning of it when the question itself tore from her a sound that was not quite a sob, not quite a laugh. *Was she badly hurt?* No, not truly. Her body was merely bruised, so what did it matter that her heart was broken and her pride was shattered and her guards were—

Flora sucked in a pained breath as the grief that she'd forced herself to suppress swept over her again. She hadn't allowed herself to think of the slaughter that morning, afraid that if she gave in to the horror of the memory, her terror would overwhelm her strength and render her helpless.

"My guards?" she whispered. "Did any live?"

She had no true hope. Not after what she'd seen done to them. Still, the shake of Brom's head laid even false hope to rest and knotted her throat with tears. "Were any other people killed? By other ogres—or along the way?"

"They only came for you."

That was a relief…for now. "They intend to start a war."

Grimly he nodded, as if the news held no surprise. Yet he said nothing more of it. A man of few words, Brom preferred to speak through his actions…which was just one of many aspects of his character that Flora had always admired. Apparently even while heartbroken, she admired it.

Now Brom looked to her bindings and showed her his blade—silently seeking permission to cut the ropes. This time she didn't cringe away. Instead she savored the gentleness of his fingers at her ankles, and the breath that hissed between his teeth when he saw her raw and bleeding wrists. It was foolish of her to cherish such moments, but Flora simply could not bear any more pain this night—and the gods knew, she would likely never know his touch again.

Though she was mistaken in that, too. When she attempted to stand, her newly-unbound legs refused to cooperate. Brom caught her before she stumbled into an ungainly heap, sweeping her up into his arms.

And he was *so* warm. The summer night had only just begun to dispel the daytime heat, yet as Brom carried Flora away from the roaring fire and into the shadows between the trees, the events of the past hours settled coldly into her flesh. She began to shiver, her teeth chattering. With a soft curse, Brom gathered her even tighter to his chest, his bare skin like a furnace against hers. Instinctively she burrowed closer, arms wrapped around his neck, her face buried against the side of his throat and her heart painfully swollen.

She'd sometimes fantasized that Brom might hold her thus. Though not in circumstances like *this*. A dream come true, in the midst of a nightmare…and all while she was awake.

A few hundred paces into a forest, a quiet nicker greeted them. Brom's big sorrel stallion waited, his tall and heavy outline barely discernible in the dark. Flora's lighter gray gelding stood nearby, and relief ballooned through her chest. When the ogres had finally stopped at the clearing and dragged her from his back, the terrified gelding had broken loose and fled into the night—likely heading toward home, so Brom must have come across her horse going the other direction and caught him.

Brom paused beside his stallion. His voice was but a rough murmur against her hair. "Can you stand?"

She did not wish to. Flora never wanted to leave his arms. Yet they could not stay here, not so near to the border between her uncle's kingdom and the ogres' lands. Brom had easily killed two of the giants, but he might not fare so well against a clan.

Reluctantly she nodded, hoping rather than knowing that her legs would support her. Brom slowly lowered her feet to the forest floor. His large hands remained at her waist while she tested the steadiness of her stance—and if Flora hadn't had evidence of his rejection, she might have believed that he lingered so long for the pleasure of touching her, not merely to make certain she wouldn't fall again.

But she knew better. "I am well," she whispered, still shivering, though her teeth no longer clacked so violently.

His expression was lost to the shadows and his eyes were but a gleam in the night. Yet she thought his gaze must hold that deceptive tenderness as he reached for a pale cloth that had been draped over his saddle. It unfurled into a tunic—no doubt discarded before he'd approached the ogres, since the white linen would have exposed him, whereas his darker skin and leather breeches would not.

"Hold still."

So that he could pull the tunic over her head. Brom's scent suddenly surrounded her and she breathed in the strong odor of sweat and horse, with tears starting to her eyes—for that was the wondrous scent of her rescue, of the hours Brom had ridden in pursuit.

Her throat aching with the gratitude that no words could ever fully express, Flora maneuvered her sore arms into the sleeves. Barely had her fingers poked through when Brom pressed a waterskin and a strip of dried venison into her hands.

"Eat," he commanded quietly. "And stay here. I need my axe and sword."

In case any more ogres came upon them. Flora nodded, not wishing to be left behind while he retrieved his weapons from the clearing, but understanding there was little choice. As she waited for his return, she drank her fill of the water and devoured the salty venison in four ravenous bites.

Just like the ogres meant to do to me, was the thought that came unbidden, and she choked silently on the near-hysterical laughter that the day's horror had rattled free from the depths.

Her breath was still hitching when Brom returned. She could almost see his frown through the dark, felt his utter stillness when he cupped her jaw in both hands and discovered the tears that had wet her cheeks.

"Flora?" he asked, his voice oddly hoarse. "What made you cry?"

"I am well," she answered shakily. "It has simply been…a very long day."

"So it has been." His thumbs stroked away her tears. "And not over yet. We must ride."

Flora nodded into his palms. She knew they must away—yet still Brom surprised her when he lifted her astride his stallion.

Immediately she protested. "My horse—"

"Is spent."

That was true. The ogres had set a brutal pace from the hunting grounds to the borderlands, and her poor gelding stood with his head drooping and exhaustion apparent in every line of his body. He could walk, but it would be a cruelty to ride him.

Yet Brom's mount had come the same distance just as quickly. "And your stallion is *not* spent?"

"Hardly." Brom moved to the gelding and stripped off his saddle, discarding it on the ground before gathering up the reins to use as a lead. "Mine was raised on the steppes of the Dead Lands."

The same harsh and unyielding wasteland that had once been home to the Stoneheart clan—a wasteland that had produced warriors as strong and as tireless as Brom's stallion.

Warriors who were truly stonehearted.

Familiar agony wrenched open her chest as Brom swung up into the saddle behind her. His arm circled her waist and pulled her back snugly against his solid torso before nudging the stallion into a walk. Another dream fulfilled.

Oh, but her dreams were so foolish. She'd *known* they were foolish. He'd all but told her they were. Because she'd *asked* him. A few weeks past, they'd been out on a hunt and she'd teasingly asked whether the people of the Stoneheart clan truly had hearts of stone.

Brom had replied, quite seriously, that they did.

But she'd laughed, convinced by his tender looks that his heart could not be so very hard, and said that his stone heart must be made of the soft, white rock that formed the Chalk Hills.

That suggestion had clearly amused him—then he'd assured her that his heart was made of granite.

Flora hadn't understood then that Brom hadn't been joking. Yet he *had* warned her. So all this pain and misery was her own fault, and she had only herself and her own silly dreams to blame.

But she couldn't bear to dwell on it. Not with him so close. Desperately she tried to think of something, *anything* else.

At least speaking of the Dead Lands and the Stoneheart clan gave her somewhere to start. "Your warriors aren't with you?"

"I am likely an hour or two ahead of them. We'll make camp for the night when they catch up to us."

When there would be safety in numbers. Of course, that was also why she'd traveled with a half-dozen guards.

She swallowed past the ache in her throat. "How did you learn I'd been taken?"

"I rode out this morning to join your hunt."

Oh gods. "And you came across—"

A slaughter.

"Yes." His arm tightened around her and his voice took on that thick and ragged edge again. "I lost a short time searching for you before I realized none of the remains were yours. I sent word to my warriors and to Vash—then began following the trail."

And he must have set a pace as brutal as the ogres had. "Thank you," she whispered unsteadily, clutching the steely forearm locked across her middle. "Even ten minutes later and…"

He'd have found her haunch, instead. And her head. And her ring.

But no need to say that. They both knew what the outcome would have been if Brom hadn't arrived when he did. For a long moment, the nighttime noise of the forest and the steady clop of hooves seemed to press down heavily around them.

Then Brom drew in a harsh breath and cut through the oppressive quiet. "Only yesterday, it seemed that little could be worse than your avoidance of me. But coming across your hunting party was worse. Knowing the ogres had you was worse."

Flora knew not what to say. She only knew that the flicker of hope that rose in her breast was a fool's hope and desperately tried to quash it. Just because he'd wanted her company didn't mean he wanted *her.*

He'd said it himself. Never could he accept her. *Never.* "Why have you not looked at me these past days?" Frustration burned through each word. "What have I done?"

He'd refused her hand. But Flora could hardly explain how devastating his rejection had been. Not without exposing her shattered heart…and she had a little bit of pride left. So she could only shake her head, squeezing her eyes shut against the tears that threatened.

"Or was it your uncle? Did he command you away from me?" His voice hardened. Another shiver raced over her skin when she felt his hot breath against her cheek, but her trembling became icy stillness as he lowered his mouth to her ear and said with quiet viciousness, "He will marry you off—*sell* you off—to the magic-wielders."

In the kingdom south of Innis, which no one from the Dead Lands would ever align themselves with. For in an age past, it had been sorcerers who'd tipped the scales so far out of balance with their corrupted magic that a Reckoning had swept through the once-fertile lands, devastating the realm. For generations upon generations, Innis never had aligned itself with magicians, either. Flora could not understand how any kingdom so near to the Dead Lands would, knowing that history. But she supposed memories were often short—and fear or greed made such consequences even easier to forget.

And her uncle feared Innis would fall to the ogres. So it was true, her uncle likely would sell her off as a bride—if not to the sorcerers, then some other realm that he wished to make an alliance with. Flora hadn't been useful to him in securing the Stoneheart clan, so he would make use of her with the next.

Her chest felt hollow. "It is my duty."

"Your *duty?*" Brom spat the words back as if they tasted foul upon his tongue.

"He took me in after my parents succumbed to the blue fever, kept me safe and secure," she recited dully. "It is what I owe to him and to our people, to keep them safe and secure in return."

"This is what he has told you?"

"For most of my life." And Flora could not argue with it. She *did* owe him. After her cousin Vash, she was next in line to the royal throne. Her uncle could have sent her away or killed her, as many kings did to their potential rivals. Instead he'd taken her in.

"And what of *his* duty?"

"His?" she echoed in confusion.

"To see you happy. Or to at least keep his promise of making you safe and secure. Or does that promise only hold until he marries you off? For the price of feeding and clothing a child, he would take possession of the remainder of your life and trade you to another kingdom when it suits him." A low growl reverberated through his chest. "You are worth so much more than that."

Burning tears threatened to fall. Desperately she held them back. "To be fair to my uncle, the price of my clothing is *quite* expensive."

She attempted to say it lightly, yet her breath still hitched and her voice still broke. Perhaps Brom recognized that she jested in order to deflect the overwhelming impact of his words, because he merely eased back, and his only response was to briefly tighten the embrace of his arm around her waist.

You are worth so much more than that.

Her eyes squeezed shut. Never would she be worth more to her uncle. So he would soon try to marry her off again.

And yet…What if she refused to marry at her uncle's—the *king's*—command?

With that rebellious thought, a strange little hope flared to life inside her. Because she probably *could* refuse. After all, her uncle had not taken her in out of the kindness of his heart—he'd taken her in due to the kindness of her parents' hearts. Generous and merciful, they'd been beloved by everyone within the kingdom and their deaths were deeply mourned. Violently removing Flora from the royal line would have risked the wrath and hatred of the people under her uncle's rule.

And Flora had continued her parents' traditions as best she could. As a member of the royal family, she was one of the few who could hunt wild game without being arrested for poaching. But the meat she hunted never ended up on the king's table—instead she brought it each day to villages and families in need. For that, she was as beloved as her parents had been. So her uncle might not risk angering the kingdom by marrying her off against her will or severely punishing Flora for her disobedience if she refused.

Though if it came to that, she might simply…leave. Go to another kingdom, where she could live as quietly and as happily as she could. Which might not be very happy at first. Not until her broken heart healed. But surely one day, it would.

Perhaps such a life was not all she'd dreamed, but the possibility of it gave her much more hope than she'd had only an hour ago, when she'd seemed destined to be the ogres' feast. And it gave her more hope than she'd had even ten minutes ago, when the future that lay ahead seemed so loveless and bleak, married off for her uncle's ambitions.

By questioning her duty, Brom had opened Flora's eyes to a better future than she might have had—even if he hadn't wanted the future she'd once dreamed of sharing with him.

Never would she hope for *that* future again.

But the present was an unexpected gift to be treasured. In all the time they'd spent together, Flora had never been as close to Brom as she was now. With her back flush against his chest and her legs dangling the length of his, her body was ensconced in his solid strength and penetrating warmth. The steady rhythm of the stallion's stride kept them rocking together in slow, constant motion—and never had Flora been so aware of anything as she was each brush of his hair-roughened skin against hers, of his heated breaths lifting delicate strands from her tangled mane and feathering them across her cheek, of the enormous span of his left hand at her side and how his widespread fingers held her from hip to ribs, with his thumb nestled under the soft curve of her breast. Each moment seemed faceted by emotion and sparkling with sensation, as if every second was a flawless jewel that one day she might take out from the velvet box of her memory and examine. After only a short time in his arms, she was already wealthy beyond measure.

Then Brom shattered her peace when he quietly asked, "Did your uncle order you away from me?"

Flora closed her eyes, her throat tightening. She hadn't answered this question before. Instead she'd spoken of duty. But he'd apparently not forgotten that she'd never explained why she'd avoided him.

Mutely, she shook her head—praying he would not ask for a reason.

But he did. "Why stay away, then?" And when she could only shake her head again, he asked gruffly, "Are we not friends?"

Only friends. Oh gods, that should not hurt so much. Being friends ought to be enough—and Flora knew she was a poor friend, because she wanted too much.

But she would take whatever Brom wanted to give, and she would never ask for more.

"Yes," she said with a painful rasp in her throat. "We

are friends."

A harsh exhalation gusted past her cheek. Brom's rigid form sagged a little behind her, as if that heavy breath had released some undefined tension within him. Yet nothing about him softened; instead he pulled her even closer and buried his face in her hair for another long breath before a gentle nudge guided her upper body slightly to the side, as if he wished for her to pillow her head on his shoulder.

That she would do, and cherish every precious moment. With a contented sigh, Flora melted back against him.

Yet apparently Brom did not mean for her to sleep. "Take the reins," he ordered with such guttural urgency that Flora didn't hesitate to comply. "I will wait no longer for the next winding."

The next what? But the question died in her throat when his right hand gripped the back of her neck, his fingers tangling in the hair at her nape and tilting her head at an angle that allowed his mouth to hover just above hers.

Surprise parted her lips on a gasp that drew in his humid breath. Her heart desperately cried for him to cross the scant distance that remained.

"Flora?" Her name had never been spoken before in such deep tones that a delicious rumble echoed through her flesh. "I can begin?"

She knew not what Brom meant to start—but little did it matter. Her pulse thundering, she uttered a breathless,

"You can. *Please.*"

The rough sound Brom made as his mouth claimed hers was yet another treasure for her velvet memory box, though not a jewel that sparkled and gleamed. If a gemstone, that ravenous groan was uncut and unpolished, as if freshly carved out of the raw heart of a mountain. Her answering whimper from low in her throat was a trapped explosion of relief and joy. He did not kiss her as if this was their first, soft and searching. Instead Brom kissed her as if he'd been waiting these two months for a taste of her lips, and couldn't stop himself from devouring her in deep, hungry licks.

Slowly, his hand rose from her side to cup her breast in his palm, his thumb sweeping over the sensitive tip. A quake of pleasure raced through her body. At her shiver, Brom lifted his head. In the dark, his eyes were hooded shadows, his voice thick and full.

"I can touch you like this?"

"You can do," she panted, "anything you wish."

His quiet growl of approval was yet another memory to tuck away. And his wish must have been to kiss her more lightly, more teasingly—or he did so merely to better gauge the effect of his touch. A flick of his tongue, a toe-curling pinch. Gentle suction upon her upper lip, the rasp of calluses over softer skin. Her senses reeled under the dual onslaught of his mouth and his fingers, as his right hand held her still for his kisses and his left ignited a raging fire within her flesh.

A shudder wracked her from deep inside when his big hand smoothed downward over her belly.

Brom paused, his ragged breaths hot and harsh against her lips. "Yes?"

Her only response was to kiss him hungrily, desperately—then go utterly still as his fingers delved under linen and found heated flesh drenched in her need.

A groan ripped from his throat, reverberating through their kiss. "*Such* a wet cunt," he gritted out as if tortured by such unmistakeable evidence of her lust. His fingers began to circle her clitoris, and Flora was lost—lost to everything but the lush ecstasy that bloomed brighter with every stroke of his fingertips, everything but Brom's voice urging her higher as her back began to slowly arch, as if bracing against the explosion to come.

And when it did, he claimed her mouth hungrily again, devouring her scream as she writhed and shook in his arms. Never had her own touch wrecked her so thoroughly. Never had she dreamed any touch *could*. She clung to him, drawing out the pleasure, wishing it would never end. Yet of course it must. Gradually his kisses gentled, leaving her with lips swollen and body limp.

His mouth trailed along her jaw. "I have dreamed of doing that since the moment we met."

Another sweet memory to tuck away. Perhaps one that would hurt more later, when she examined how he wanted her yet didn't want her *enough*…but for now exhaustion combined with satisfaction and allowed her no more than a humming agreement in response.

A sigh moved through her when he withdrew his hand from between her thighs—and she drew in a sharper breath when he brought his fingers to his mouth to lick the wetness away. He made a rumbling sound of pleasure, then met her widened eyes.

"I would taste you more deeply when we make camp."

Her heart leapt. She wanted that. She'd dreamed of that. And perhaps they had been foolish dreams…but she could not pass up the opportunity for more time with him, to make more precious memories. No matter how much more it would hurt later.

Jerkily she nodded. Then managed to say, "So I'll be eaten up tonight, after all."

A breath hissed through his teeth. "*Never* will I be able to jest about that. Not when I came so near to losing—"

He broke off, clutching her tighter to his chest, burying his face in her hair. Flora bit her lip, wondering if she should take her words back when she felt the telltale shaking of his chest and the silent huffs of laughter against her ear.

"You destroy me so easily, Flora," he finally said, then pressed a kiss to her temple before wrapping his arm around her waist and taking the reins. "Rest now."

Smiling, she eased back against him and pillowed her head against his shoulder. She would rest, but wouldn't sleep. Not for anything would she miss a moment of this night—the only night she would have before they reached home. Only one night to gather up as many memories as she could hold.

Then she'd have to let him go.

2

They were still riding through the forest when the Stoneheart warriors caught up to them in a thunder of hoofbeats, their horses lathered and snorting. A few of the warriors wore leather armor over their tunics and breeches; all were armed with axes and blades.

Ready for battle—but the battle was already over. Flora couldn't mistake their relief when the glow of their torches revealed her astride Brom's mount, alive and unharmed.

Yet Flora had expected to see one other with them. "Did my cousin not come?"

She was answered by Erra, Brom's second-in-command.

"Prince Vash remains with your king." Her piercing gaze shifted to Brom and her voice seemed heavy with meaning as she added, "He awaits your message."

"Tell him that Flora is safe," Brom said, his arm securely around her waist as if to reinforce how safe she was. "I will take her home—but let him know that the Stoneheart clan will never claim King Martas as a friend."

Flora's heart constricted. But she could not even draw breath to protest before Erra had turned her horse on a tight rein and set off, flanked by two other warriors.

"Flora needs rest," Brom said to the others, and was told that a stream and clearing lay not far ahead. A few rode on at a quicker pace to set up camp, while Brom and Flora—leading her exhausted gray gelding—continued at a walk.

Finally she found her voice, but mindful of the warriors around them, spoke for his ears only. "Innis cannot defend against the ogres. Not alone. And they *do* intend to start a war. My uncle was not mistaken in that."

She was living proof of their intentions. And only because Brom had arrived in time, otherwise she'd have been dead proof.

"We will speak on it tomorrow," he replied quietly. "If we begin now, no rest would we get this night, for there is too much to explain—but I vow to you that your people will be protected."

Never would Brom speak a promise that he wouldn't keep. Flora was certain of that. She was not so persuaded as to the other reason he gave. "I did not think you intended to let me rest when we make camp. You spoke of tasting me, instead."

"You'll be on your back with your legs wrapped around my head. That seems a fair way to rest. You need not exert any effort at all, except to hold in your screams when I make you come."

Flora snickered. Then the image he'd painted hit her, and anticipation drew her nerves taut.

That tension heightened as they arrived at the camp, where the warriors had already set up a single round tent made of hide, surrounded by an array of bedrolls. Flora bathed in the cool stream, rinsing leaves and dirt from her hair, and only accepted a clean tunic because it was another of Brom's. While she sat by the fire drying her hair and eating her fill of bread, cheese, and freshly roasted rabbit, Brom tended to the raw abrasions around her wrists, applying a salve and carefully wrapping them in strips of linen. Yet each moment she was thinking of her bed, and his mouth, and the screams she'd have to hold in.

Then Brom rose to his feet and held out his hand. With her heart pounding wildly, Flora took it.

He led her to the tent, but her gaze lingered on the bedrolls around it. "They'll be outside?"

"Except in rain or snow, we prefer the open sky."

"But your furs are inside?"

"They are."

"How did they know to put your bedding there?"

Brom grinned and swept open a flap of hide, then ducked his head to enter. "They have seen me look at you."

Flora had seen him look at her, too. So many times. And she'd mistaken some of those looks, particularly the tender ones—but there was no mistaking the hunger in his expression before the tent enclosed them in a darkness that was only broken where the firelight slipped between the seams.

"And your lips are still swollen from my kisses." His voice dropped as he moved in closer, cupping her face in his hands. "I would kiss you again, Flora."

"I would allow it any time." Though she would only have this one night. "On my mouth or anywhere else."

She felt his quiet laugh against her lips, then there was only his mouth, and his tongue, and heat rushing through her flesh. In her dreams alone had she imagined kissing could be like this—so wild and world-consuming, so that every sensation his touch evoked was as sharp as a knife's edge…and yet there was nothing beyond the walls of their tent, as if all the rest of the world had vanished.

Did Brom feel anything near to the same as she did? But he could not. How could *anyone* feel like this and then reject it?

Unless their heart was made of stone. As Brom had said his was.

With a sobbing hitch to her breath, Flora clung to his shoulders. Then ran her palms down his chest, desperately touching the skin that after this night she'd never feel again, the wonderful steel of his muscles and the crisp rasp of hair, the rapid thrum of his heart that beat ever faster when her hand slid down to grip the thick column of flesh straining the leather of his breeches.

His hips jerked, thrusting that hot length against her palm. With a tortured groan, Brom broke away from her mouth, his chest heaving ragged breaths. "Don't touch— It's too— I can't—" His forehead pressed to hers for an endless, burning second. "I've needed you for too long, Flora. I'll spend into your hand."

"Then I'll lick your come from my fingers as you did mine."

A growl ripped from his chest. The world spun, then she was on her back, in his furs. Brom's mouth devoured hers. His hands dragged at the tunic, baring her thighs, baring her breasts. His heavy body pinned her as he licked his way down her throat, though she squirmed and fought to touch more of him, to taste more of him—so focused on the battle that the pleasure of his teeth tugging at her nipple shocked from her a startled cry.

Instantly Brom was over her again, his thumb pressing between her parted lips, quietly hushing into her ear. "I would share everything with my clan but this," he said in a voice as hard and thick as the rampant erection cradled between her thighs. "Your pleasure is mine alone. Yes?"

Flora nodded, then sucked on the tip of his thumb. Brom stiffened above her before parrying with a roll of his hips that ground his rigid cock against her most intimate flesh. Barely did she stop her cry, whimpering instead low in her throat.

"Just like that, Flora," he said huskily. "Mine alone."

His alone. She buried her fingers in the thickness of his hair as he returned to her breasts, desperately trying to remain quiet as his mouth teased her tight nipples from sensitive to aching, so that the gentlest pinch of his teeth and slick of his tongue brought her near to screaming.

It was both relief and torment when Brom kissed his way lower—but he was slow, so slow, that she released his hair and skated her fingers down ahead of his mouth.

Again Brom surged over her, bringing her hands up with him to pin over her head. He nipped at her bottom lip. Softly he warned her, "Mine alone, Flora."

She had to laugh at that. He would claim everything but her hand in marriage.

Yet when Brom hesitated, as if he'd heard the bitter note and meant to question it, she shook her head. She would not waste this night when it was all that she would have of him. "Yours alone. Please."

His gaze searched hers before he nodded. Then he kissed her in the way that made the world disappear, until once again there was only him and her, and the havoc his mouth could raise upon her heart and her flesh. In the dim and flickering light within the tent, he was shadow and fire, burning a dark path from her lips to her stomach to her thighs—and there he paused, to breathe her in, to spread her wide, so that by the time his journey resumed, her every muscle was trembling. And it would be *this* memory that was the brightest of all the jewels, this one this one *this one*—because in the instant before he lowered his head, the way Brom looked at her seemed beyond tenderness, beyond cherishing, beyond even worship.

In that deceitful dark, Flora could almost dream that he loved her.

It could not be true. His heart was stone.

But her heart was already his, and she would take whatever he gave. Just as she took the first gentle, searching kiss that parted the folds of her cunt and laid her open to the next, and the next, and the next. Her cries she only held back with her hand to her lips, as his tongue licked and licked, hungrier with each taste, gathering her closer, gathering up more of her, until her legs were wrapped around his head and his forearm pinned her hips, because this carnal kiss was so sweet, and so good, and she couldn't stop moving, couldn't stop twisting, as if each devastating lick unleashed a hurricane of pleasure beneath her skin. A wail built with it, and when the storm broke even biting her fist could not contain her scream—but Brom was there, surging over her again, drawing into himself everything he'd given her, his kiss deep and shattering.

Yet there was more. Because his hand worked between them, ripping at the leather lacing his breeches. Groaning, he shoved between her legs, grinding his cock against the sodden heat of her cunt—then stilled as his body was racked with violent shudders.

Hot seed spilled over her lower belly. As if Brom, even as big and strong as he was, simply couldn't contain it. Suddenly laughing into his kiss, Flora wrapped her arms around his heaving shoulders.

When their breathing slowed, Brom lifted his head and gave her an abashed look. "I had no intention of doing that."

She grinned. "I rather enjoyed it."

And enjoyed it even more when Brom rolled to his side and slid his fingers through the seed pooled on her belly, then slipped down to the wetness between her thighs. Still sensitive, she bit her lip—and found him watching her face with all the tenderness in his eyes that she'd mistaken before.

Until the morning came, she would let herself believe in it.

His gaze searched hers. "Do you wish me to stay with you this night?"

This night. She wanted him forever. But this night was what she'd been given.

"I do," she said softly.

In response, he kissed her mouth, then used his discarded tunic to clean her off before gathering her into his arms. Flora lay her head over his stone heart and held on tight. Tomorrow he would take her home.

Somehow, she had to make this night last her for the rest of her life.

3

Given so little time to spend with him, Flora hadn't meant to sleep. Yet she must have, because she awoke to the decadent pleasure of Brom leisurely feasting upon her cunt. She had but a moment to admire him in the pale morning light, his dark hair tangled and his mouth reddened and glistening with her wet lust— then his tongue slicked over her clit, and ecstasy rolled through her veins in a long, hot wave. She choked on a cry, then crammed her fist against her mouth, her body undulating with each slow, scorching lick until Brom had to hold her down again, and then she could do nothing but come and come and come.

He made his way back up slowly, kissing a path to her mouth where he settled in for another long and leisurely taste. But eventually the noise from outside had to intrude—his warriors were readying the horses and waiting to take down the tent.

And so this sweet dream had to end.

His gaze narrowed when she squeezed her eyes shut and turned her head away. "Should I not have awakened you by kissing your cunt? Have I angered you?"

"No!" Never could she let him think so. "Anywhere, anytime. I meant it. I am merely…"

A dreaming fool.

His brow furrowed. "Do you still worry about the ogres?"

"I do." At least that was true.

A muscle worked in his jaw. "Do you still intend to fulfill your duty to your uncle?"

"No," she said quietly, and his eyes widened.

"I am glad of it." He brushed a curl from her cheek. "We have much to speak of. We will ride together again."

On his stallion. So this was not yet the end. Not until they reached her uncle's palace. With a hesitant smile, Flora swiftly kissed his mouth. The next minutes were spent donning clothes, rolling up his furs, and finding any excuse to touch him—all with her heart full, so *stupidly* full, because such fullness would only hurt all the more when it was punctured again.

They set out again at an easy walking pace, though

with one of Brom's warriors leading her gray gelding. She spent the first minutes watching her horse for any signs of lameness or strain—but aside from lingering fatigue that rest and grain ought to cure, he seemed well enough.

Though…they were going the wrong way.

She glanced at the sun to be certain. "We are headed east."

"We are."

Toward his clan's territory? "Your message to Vash said that you're taking me home."

"I am. To *my* home. And now your home. You'll be safe there."

Longing pierced her heart. But it could not be. "I won't abandon Innis. I may not be of much use in a war against the ogres, but I can be of *some* use."

"There will be no war. The ogres are no threat to you or to Innis. The threat to you comes from another direction."

A disbelieving laugh escaped her. "Did you forget already how you found me last eve? And what the ogres' intentions were?"

"Yesterday you were terrified and had no time to think. So think on it now."

She forgot, now and then, how Brom sometimes irritated the piss out of her. *Think on it?* What was there to think? Her uncle had long believed that ogres were planning to destroy Innis. At one point, he'd argued that Innis ought to strike first, marching into the mountains and routing the ogres out of their caves—only to have his son, his generals, and his councilors advise him to wait, as Innis's defenses were stronger than an army advancing into unknown territory would be. Which was why her uncle had been so desperate to form an alliance with the Stoneheart clan; whether striking out or defending, the warriors' strength would improve Innis's chances either way.

When Flora had been taken, her uncle had been proved right…except the ogres hadn't attacked the kingdom. Instead only two had tried to provoke Innis into declaring war on the ogres.

Nausea suddenly churned in her gut. "You think my uncle *hired* them to start a war?"

"So does your cousin."

That could not surprise her. "Vash was always of the opinion that the evidence my uncle gave of the upcoming attack seemed slight. And *I* was always of the opinion that I was safe from him. That is why he took me in, and would have married me off—so he could make use of me in a way that wouldn't enrage the rest of Innis. Instead he hoped to enrage them so they'd *demand* to go to war?"

"Yes."

She gave a sick, hollow laugh. "No wonder he proposed marrying me to you. He knew that you would have led the Stoneheart clan into the mountains yourself if the ogres had eaten your betrothed. Is that why you rejected the proposal?"

"No. I would have always refused such a marriage."

Her heart shriveled. "Oh."

"Vash and I had not imagined then that your uncle would use you in such a way." His voice suddenly roughened. "Flora?"

"I am well." She hastily wiped away the tears that had dripped onto his forearm. But her response was hardly more than a croak and he would know it for a lie. Pressing her palm to her mouth, she tried not to sob, but it seemed a long time before she could trust herself to speak, and still it emerged on broken breaths. "Was there more to the message than was said?"

His arm around her tightened its embrace. "To Vash?"

She nodded.

He hesitated for a moment. "It was exactly as I said. The Stoneheart clan will never be friends to King Martas."

But Brom *was* friends with Vash. And Brom had vowed that Innis would be protected.

Oh. "Vash will kill my uncle and take the crown?"

"He will."

Probably for the best. "He did not ask for your support?"

"Not when it might seem as if the Stoneheart clan had betrayed the offer of friendship that your uncle extended."

And so that no one would wonder whether Brom had made a puppet of Vash after he claimed the throne. "I see. What was it that my uncle had hoped to gain by marching an army into the mountains?" Oh, but she could answer that herself. "The mines. It is said they are filled with jewels and gold, which the ogres care nothing about."

"Two did."

"True." Because her uncle must have paid two to kill her. And now…what was she to do? "So you are taking me out of my uncle's reach."

"I am."

"So I am to wait until all is settled before I return to Innis?"

Brom stiffened behind her. "You wish to return? Did I not please you?"

"I… I don't—" Her lips smashed tight as tears threatened again.

His voice was harsh. "By the wetness of your cunt as you came, you seemed well pleased. So I will continue to court you."

"Court me?" Pain ripped a bitter laugh from her chest. "You already rejected me."

"*Never* would I reject you," he snarled.

"I heard you! In the meeting with my uncle—"

"That was no rejection of *you*. I rejected that marriage. Never could I accept such."

Had she gone mad? Did words make no sense? "I don't understand."

Brom caught her chin to tilt her head back against his shoulder, confusion creasing his brow as he studied her face—as if baffled by *her* confusion. "Never would any of our clan marry to secure an alliance. Marriage is only for love."

Her lips parted as his words filled her with hope, so much hope, yet she could not be foolish again. "For love?

But your hearts are stone!"

"As they should be," he said, brow still furrowed. "Is your heart not?"

"No! I wish it was!" Then it could never have shattered. "How can you speak of love if your heart is too hard to let it in? Wouldn't your heart be impervious to love?"

A slow smile curved his mouth. "How can you speak of love if you believe a heart is soft and weak?" Brom tossed back, then abruptly he laughed. "Like chalk. That is what you meant? I believed it a jest when you said my heart must be akin to a soft, white stone. Is that what you wish? To share a love that will easily crumble in your fist?"

"No, I… I…" She suddenly felt dizzy, as if the entire world had shifted under her feet.

"Love," he said quietly, "is the strongest of all true magics. Trust that it can penetrate anything. Even stone. But what my heart will *not* do is easily crumble. A stone heart will weather any troubles, just as a mountain stands against storm and quake. With time enough, perhaps my heart might wear away…but that time would be far longer than I am ever likely to live."

"Oh," she whispered.

"But you thought elsewise? You thought that I couldn't love—and that I'd refused you? So you kept away from me."

Flora could not answer. Not without sobbing.

"Yet still you let me touch you. Though I'd hurt you so badly, still you would have taken more and given as much in return." He brushed a tear from her cheek. "Such a heart you have, already to have withstood so much. Stronger even than granite—a diamond, sharp and clear."

That couldn't be. "It broke," she confessed on a shuddering breath.

"Did it? And all the love spilled out, gone forevermore?"

"No." None of it had gone. "Though these past days might have been less painful if it had."

His eyes darkened. "Forgive me for that."

"For a misunderstanding?"

"For not being clear in my intention. Never would I have hurt you. I thought you understood that I meant to have you."

"I thought I understood, too," she replied quietly. "All the time we spent together, the way you looked at me… but then I heard you refuse me."

"Then I ought to have said more and not forced you to rely on looks." His brows drew together in a frown. "Yet surely you must have known my intention when you accepted the second winding?"

"I don't know what that is. I just wanted to kiss you."

That earned her another kiss—swift and hard—before he eyed her with some bafflement again. "How can you not know the windings? The marriage ritual is the same in Innis as in the Dead Lands."

"Binding hands with a red ribbon and speaking vows?"

"That is the wedding. But courtship is marked by the winding of the ribbon around each finger—first with friendship, then passion in all its forms, followed by shared values and hopes, a stone heart to withstand all troubles, and a promise to care for each other and any children that may come." With each one, Brom mimed winding a ribbon around Flora's fingers, then finished with a full loop around her hand. "Then love binds all together in marriage."

"Never have I heard that before."

Not letting go of her hand, Brom intertwined his fingers with hers. "Perhaps it has fallen out of tradition in places where they marry for other than love."

Her heart beat faster. "So we had established friendship. And the second—"

"Is the bed." His thumb stroked a circle in the center of her palm, making her shiver. "Though some start with passion and find friendship later. But though I wished for both, I thought your uncle and cousin would not allow me to begin your courtship in bed."

Flora would not have argued against it. "So you wish to bed me before we marry? To make certain our passion is well-matched?"

"I know our passions are matched. I knew before I ever kissed you."

Flora had also thought so. Or hoped so.

And perhaps those hopes were not so foolish, after all. "But I would like to have you in my bed soon, anyway. To be certain."

His grin matched hers, too. "The moment we are home. When I take you the first time, I would not have you muffle your screams."

"How long must we ride before we reach Stoneheart lands?"

"Five days at this pace."

She groaned. But perhaps it would not be so terrible—and they could begin the next winding in the courtship, as well, and speak of their values and goals… though in truth, after all that she'd learned of him in the past months, she was certain they were already aligned. Brom had accompanied her on so many hunts, then to the villages where she helped her people as best she could. He knew that of her, and of all that she hoped to accomplish—and had openly admired her for it. In turn, she'd seen the respect his warriors paid him and heard their stories about Brom's leadership of their clan.

Yes, she believed they were quite closely aligned in purpose and values, even if their focus and activities were often different. Yet she wouldn't regret taking a few more days speaking of them and being certain.

But those were the days. During the nights… "Will we still share a tent?"

"We will."

"And you will allow me to touch you and kiss you?"

"Any time. My mouth, and anywhere else."

Her delighted laugh rang out. "But you will have to muffle your screams, warrior. Your pleasure is mine alone."

"Yours alone." Brom squeezed her hand and held her tight. Solemnly he added, "*Always* yours alone."

4

Flora had heard both Vash and Brom describe the fortress held by the Stoneheart clan—yet nothing could have prepared her for the towering stronghold rising above the sheer face of the granite cliffs, or the crystalline waterfalls that filled the air with rainbows of sparkling mist. Horses grazed green terraced pastures, children chased each other shrieking with laughter, and everywhere she looked, joy seemed in no short supply.

"Do you think you could be happy here?" Brom murmured in her ear as they rode the long winding ribbon of cobblestones that led to the stronghold.

"I think I would have to exert every effort *not* to be happy here—and still I might fail."

He brushed a kiss against her temple before straightening again, calling out greetings here and there. Despite the curious looks Flora received, Brom didn't pause to introduce her fully, aside from proudly announcing that she was his bride. Considering the hard length nestled against her ass, Flora thought it likely that Brom wouldn't halt anywhere before they'd reached his bedchamber.

Until she said, "Do you wish to marry first?"

She must have surprised him. The stallion tossed his head, as if reacting to unexpected tension in the reins. In a flat voice, as if he didn't wish to reveal his preference either way, Brom asked, "Do you not wish to continue courting—to be certain?"

"I *am* certain." And because she hadn't declared herself so openly before, despite five blissful days and nights in his arms, she continued, "I do not wish to be in your bed simply to discover whether I can love you and want you enough to marry you—I know that I do. Love you, that is. And want you. Enough to marry. Enough to *not* marry, and still continue loving and wanting you." Except…Brom had made no declaration either, and now he sat rigidly behind her. In a smaller voice, she added, "Unless you need *me* to continue courting *you*."

Anxiously she turned her head to look back at him—and there was such tenderness in his gaze. His throat worked, and a moment later he said thickly, "I have never needed you to court me. I have wanted you from the beginning, and loved you almost as long."

Her heart might burst. "Truly?"

"Truly."

Sheer happiness bubbled through her veins as she debated their next step. "So you've been waiting longer to bed me than to marry me."

"I have."

"Well, then." Flora settled back against him again. "Your bedchamber awaits, and your heart isn't the only part of you that's hard as stone. We'll marry when you've finished making me scream."

Brom laughed and nudged the stallion into a faster gait.

No doubt the fortress was even more impressive the nearer they approached, for she'd heard of the intricate carvings and magnificent arches. Flora barely saw a thing. Because as soon as Brom rode into the courtyard and lifted her down from the saddle—and up into his arms—all the world faded away, until there was only him and her, and the way Brom kissed her as he carried her into his chambers.

Hoping for this had never been a mistake. Dreaming of him had never been foolish.

The past five days had taught her that. The greatest of all treasures was to have a friend who could set fire to her skin. Who searched out every spot that made her shiver with need, who trembled when she took him in her hand or her mouth.

And who looked at her as Brom did. Cherishing her, loving her.

Yet he did not make her rely on a look. Instead he murmured words of love as he laid her on the bed. Instead he called her beautiful, and delicious, and *his*, kissing her again from swollen lips to drenched cunt, and every quivering inch of skin between.

Such bliss it was, to be loved. So Flora gave all the love she could in return, with mouth and tongue, with words and kisses.

There another battle began, because she wanted to give more—yet Brom wanted her ready, *needed* her ready, whereas he could not be more ready without spending. This he told her, too, which made her laugh…yet the laugh lasted only as long as his next lick. Then she gripped his hair and writhed against his tongue.

And ready he made her. Wet, so wet. So slippery, she believed that her body could offer no resistance—but her barbarian was big, indeed. Big enough to make her cry out as his cock began a slow penetration, but it was his gentleness that made her scream as his thickness stretched her narrow sheath. The slight pain of taking him was nothing to the agonized frustration of needing him deeper, and deeper, and deeper, as Brom denied her every desperate entreaty. She pulled at him, and pushed at him—until finally he relented and she was full, fuller than she'd ever dreamed.

Because her dreams were nothing to the reality of feeling

him moving inside her. So deep inside her. No words did Brom need now. Always his nature was to speak through action, and never had Flora loved his nature more than when his body began to worship hers. When each touch, each kiss, each thrust told her that his only purpose was her pleasure, that she was his…and he was hers alone.

And when his every movement became rougher, harder, as his control shattered under the force of his need for her, she met him stroke for stroke, kiss for kiss. With legs wrapped around his hips, she tumbled over the edge, her spine bowed and her cunt clamping down on the throbbing shaft buried deep inside her. The flood of his seed sent another convulsion through her flesh. She clung to him, utterly full of his love—and with her heart a shining diamond in her chest. Strong. Unbreakable.

Made of stone.

Epilogue

"Do you hide from me?" asked Brom's deep, familiar voice, just before his arms circled her from behind. His big hands curved possessively over the slight swell of her belly. "Always, I will find you."

Flora laughed, angling her head back against his shoulder. "I was not hiding. I was waiting."

"I thought we were to wait in the courtyard."

To greet King Vash when he arrived. A full year had passed since Flora had arrived in Stoneheart territory, and she and Brom had been married just as long—minus the week they'd spent in bed before finally seeking out a witch to perform the wedding. In that time, Vash had deposed King Martas and taken Innis's throne—yet had remained in his kingdom to root out the councilors who were still loyal to her uncle. For a year, the only communication between the two realms had been through letters.

Now she gestured to the window, which offered a clear view of the road leading to the fortress. Her cousin rode at the head of a handful of guards, the king's banner flying at the tail. "It is easier to see his approach from this tower."

"So it is." Brom bent his head to kiss the side of her neck, and she heard the smile in his voice when she shivered in response to that warm caress. "He is still twenty minutes distant."

She smiled, knowing full well what he was thinking. "It will take ten minutes to walk down the stairs."

His hands rose to cup her breasts. "Erra will greet him if we are late."

Flora snickered, for Brom's second-in-command would greet the king, indeed—most likely with a sword and a glare. "I told him in my last letter how to properly court a warrior from the Stoneheart clan."

"It would have been more entertaining if you had not."

"Knowing Vash, it will still be entertaining." She bit her lip against a soft moan when Brom's thumbs swept over her nipples. For weeks now, her breasts had been more sensitive than ever before, and he could bring her to climax merely by suckling them.

At times it seemed he might bring her to climax merely

by *looking* at them—or by looking at her. Never had a man's gaze held so much meaning or as much emotion as Brom's always did. And not once since their marriage had Flora ever doubted what she saw. Yet still, he never made her rely on a look. Just as she no longer concealed her heart from him.

"I love you," she breathed—and was spun around, away from the window, where she might be seen. Even now, he would not share her pleasure with anyone else.

His alone.

Love burned fiercely in his eyes as Brom lifted her against the stone wall, tugging and pulling at the fastenings and clothing between them. Oh, but she loved it when he was in a rush. And loved it when he was slow. Loved it when he was sweet and when he was rough—and loved it now, when his mouth claimed hers, capturing her scream when he surged deep. Every thrust drove her higher, wilder, until the ecstasy crested and wrecked her against him, clinging to his shoulders as he poured himself into her quivering sheath.

Then he kissed her, and kissed her again. And as it always did when Brom kissed her in that way, the world outside seemed to vanish, leaving only her and him.

And a love that was so much more than she'd ever dreamed.

• END •

Pretty Bride

To anyone who's ever cut out a piece of themselves,
trying to help someone else. I see you.

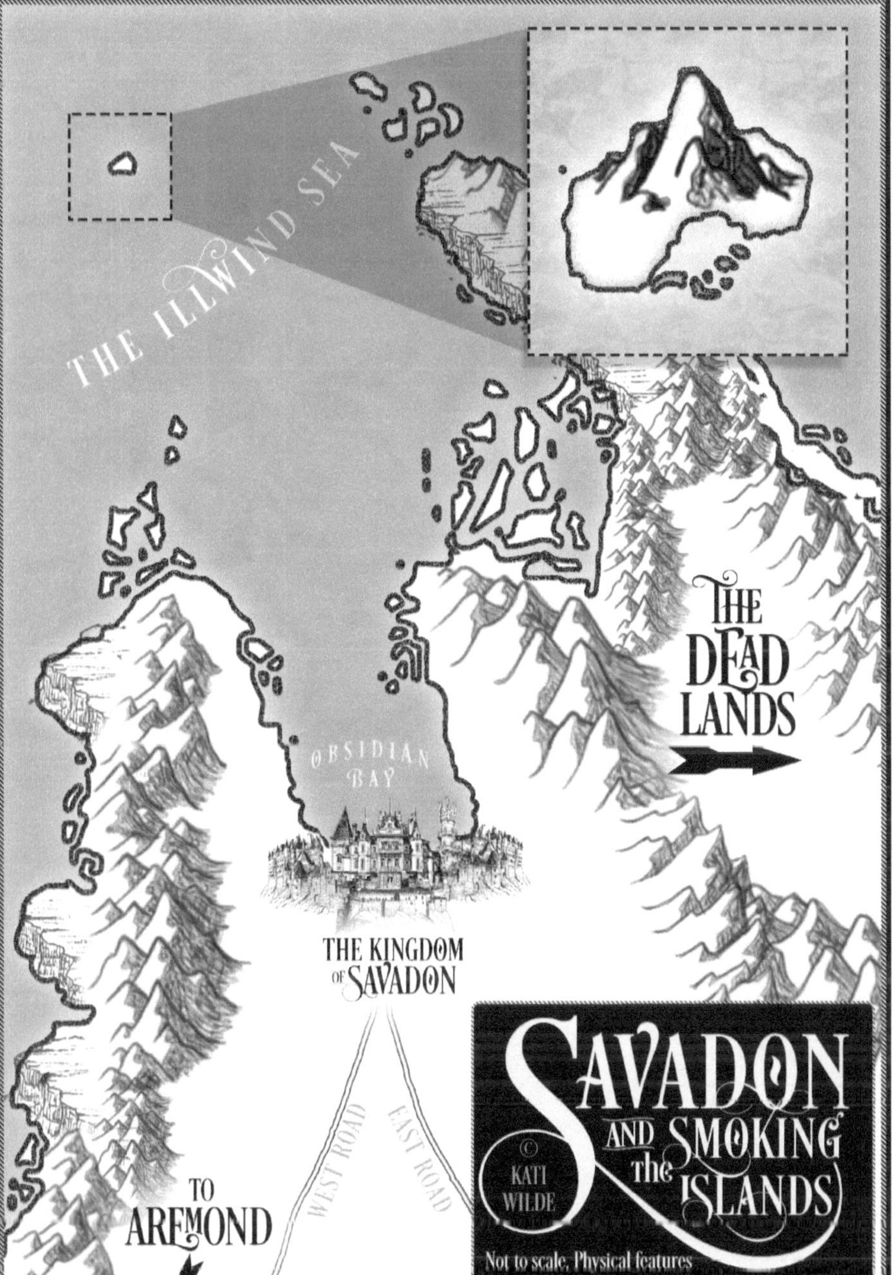

THE ILLWIND SEA
THE DEAD LANDS
OBSIDIAN BAY
THE KINGDOM OF SAVADON
TO AREMOND
WEST ROAD
EAST ROAD
SAVADON AND THE SMOKING ISLANDS
KATI WILDE
Not to scale. Physical features and distances are exaggerated for clarity and fun.

ERE WE ARE, IN THE MIDST OF THREE TALES ABOUT BRIDES of the Dead Lands, who are also called stoneheart and midnight—

But now comes the pretty bride.

The time is anotherwhen, a date unknown but only two nights before a fateful storm; the place is anotherwhere, a world unnamed but on the southern shore of the Illwind Sea. And this story begins, as many stories do, with a desperate princess wearing a smile that she doesn't feel, and a barbarian warrior too preoccupied by his long, hard sword to perceive what she conceals.

Only magic can pierce a guarded woman's skilled illusion, and our barbarian warrior is no sorcerer. Fear not, however, that this tale will end unhappily. Our hero has a skull as thick as his sword, but his heart burns bright and true.

And although love sometimes makes us bleed…it is powerful magic, too.

ARUK the LOST

Savadon

"I see Mara ahead," Aruk's brother said, his voice filled with sheer relief. "She is making her way past that fishmonger's stall."

Trying to make her way. Aruk saw her now, a slim figure with dark hair. Crowds packed these streets so tightly, she was forced to wedge herself between the people standing in her way. She was a small woman, so it ought have been easy for her to slip through, but the saddle she carried and the pack slung over her shoulder prevented easy passage.

No such trouble did Aruk and Strax have. They stood

head and shoulders above everyone around them, muscles hardened by years of hiring out their swords. People made room for the brothers, even when there was no room to make.

"Call out to her," Strax said.

"Has your voice broken?"

"If I do, she will not wait for us."

That was truth. If Aruk's brother called her name, Mara might push harder through the crowd to get away from him. Strax had made a quick enemy of her three weeks past, at the start of the tournament to retrieve Khides' gauntlet, by telling her that she wouldn't last a week on the difficult route—especially as her competition were all experienced warriors, and she an unskilled noblewoman.

Aruk had thought the same, yet he'd had the brains not to say it.

And in the past weeks, Mara had proved herself far more capable than either brother had expected. But if ever Aruk looked at a woman in the same yearning and hopeless way his brother looked at Mara of Aremond, he prayed some kind soul would take pity on him and run his heart through with a sword.

A fine woman Mara was. Yet never could his brother have her—as Strax knew well. Mara believed Strax and Aruk were contestants in this tournament, as she was. In truth, they were bound by a blood obligation to prevent anyone from claiming the prize. In the end, all the obstacles she faced and all the sacrifices she made would be for nothing. For certain, she would hate them then.

Or she would hate Aruk then. Strax, she already did.

But from the moment his brother had clapped eyes on her, his heart had been ensnared. And there were but two ways for Aruk to watch Strax's helpless tumble into love—with his heart sore and aching for his brother, or with amusement and laughter as Strax twisted himself into knots.

Aruk always chose amusement. "For what purpose should we tell her to wait? We know where she goes."

To the docks, as they did. The tournament map clearly marked the route from Aremond, where the contest had begun, to Khides' Keep, which would take at least six months of hard travel to reach. They were in Savadon now, a kingdom that served as the only port along the southern coast of the Illwind Sea. From here they would sail to the northern coast.

Frustration marked Strax's voice as Mara slipped out of sight, swallowed up again by the crowd. "She might find passage on a different ship."

And Strax would not see her again until they landed on the northern shore. His brother might suffer weeks of agony. So Aruk would amuse himself a little longer.

"She likely will, anyway. A noblewoman such as she will hire a ship we cannot afford." And had probably not needed to sell her horse, as they had. She could have afforded passage for it, as well. But finding a ship that could also board a horse might take more time, and it was easy enough to buy another mount on the north shore.

"Call to her!" Strax snarled.

Grinning, Aruk shouted over the crowd, "Mara of Aremond! Hold where you are, and my brother and I will hasten your path to the docks!"

Nothing would tempt her more than going faster. This tournament was a race, and she lagged far behind the other contestants.

Strax surged ahead, forging a path through the crowd. A laughing Aruk followed in his wake. Quickly his brother was upon her, hauling the burden of the saddle from her grip and snarling, "If you cannot even push your way through a crowd, how will you have strength enough to climb the Skull Cliffs?"

"By eating the hearts of my enemies," she snapped back. "Though I think yours might taste like piss."

"More likely troll dung," Aruk said. "Fresh and steaming."

Strax growled at both of them.

Mara held out her hand in clear demand. "Give back to me the saddle. I *can* carry it."

"You wish to go faster? Then I will carry it. Follow close behind Aruk as he makes a path."

And with Strax close behind Mara. The besotted, cursed fool. Aruk glanced back once to see his brother bending his face nearer to Mara's hair, as if to catch her scent, eyes closing in a mix of agony and ecstasy when he breathed her in.

She ignored Strax utterly. Around them, the crowd

grew restless as trumpets sounded in the distance.

She tapped his shoulder, voice lifted over the din. "The horse dealer said the primary route to the docks will be near impassable, and to cut through to the lower street after we pass through the main square."

Aruk nodded. "What is this celebration?"

"Savadon's princess has come of age, so they are gathered for a parade."

A parade for which the entire kingdom seemed to have turned out. "A popular princess, apparently."

"I do not know about that," came Mara's wry reply. "In short time, I have heard her called spoiled and selfish and difficult. So I suspect they truly gather because gold coins were minted with her likeness, and as part of the celebration, they will be tossed into the crowd."

"They toss gold at the crowd? Then I might also linger for a glimpse of this princess, spoiled and difficult though she is."

Mara laughed. "I have seen your purse. You are not so desperate for coins."

"But we will not hire out our swords while seeking the gauntlet," he said to her. "So there will be many coins leaving that purse and none going in. What sort of selfish princess tosses away gold?"

"I do not know that she is truly selfish. That is only what was said—and not much weight would I give to such words. Spoiled, she might be. Many princesses are. But I have known too many women who were called selfish and difficult, simply because those women did as they liked without regard for the opinions of those who would have her behave in a manner better suited to their own interests."

"I think you might have been called difficult a time or two."

"So I have." She sounded amused. "Though by that measure, I am not nearly as difficult as a barbarian from the Dead Lands."

As he and Strax were. "You think we only do as we like?"

"I think that you are so big that even if you were selfish and spoiled, never would I have the courage to say so aloud."

Aruk laughed, for that was a clear lie. She had courage enough to say anything to warriors of his size. Had she not just threatened to eat his brother's heart? Though there was nothing left of it that she had not already consumed.

The trumpets sounded again, nearer. The crowd surged, breaking around Aruk as a stream broke around a rock. Mara staggered into his back.

Her sharp protest sounded, then his brother's gruff, "Quiet, woman. When they begin throwing coins, you'll be trampled by the mob. I'll set you down again when we are clear of the crowd."

It was not coins yet, but the parade—mounted soldiers riding two abreast, banners flying, and those at the front shouting for everyone to make way. The crowd surged again, parting to clear a path through the street. The press of people around him became a tight crush, as they jostled for position and shoved closer together. On opposite side, he saw a woman stumble against another and disappear.

This was madness. Pushing forward, he threw back to Strax, "Get Mara away from this. I will meet you at the docks."

With Mara cradled against his chest, his brother gave a short nod and pressed on.

Aruk broke through the line and into the cleared street, paying no heed to the mounted soldier shouting at him to make way. He shoved into the crowd on the opposite side, gaze locked on where the woman had fallen. With sheer muscle, he made a path and dragged the woman up to her feet.

"Are you hurt? Shall I carry you out?"

Crying, the woman shook her head. "I wish to see our princess. A great beauty she is said to be."

This woman risked her life in this crowd to see a princess's beauty? At least the gold was worth something.

He made certain she was steady before pushing back toward the street. At the front of the crowd he was forced to wait by the passing parade. Mounted soldier after mounted soldier, then the princess herself, riding a white mare.

And a beauty she was indeed. A gold circlet crowned black curls that tumbled over her shoulders in waves. She had dainty features, from the arch of her brows to her pretty little nose and delicate chin. Her pink lips curved into a sweet smile that never faltered as she waved to the crowd shouting her name.

Princess Jalisa. Who smiled and smiled and smiled as she rode past Aruk, her eyes meeting his for a brief moment before swinging sharply back. Her gaze ran down his length and the smile vanished, revealing the fullness of her mouth in the instant before her lips pressed into a thin line.

Reining her horse around, she stopped before Aruk, regarding him imperiously from the height of her saddle. Abruptly the shouts from the crowd quieted.

"Have you no respect for a royal princess, barbarian," she said in haughty voice, "that you arrive bare to my parade and flaunt yourself before me?"

Aruk was not bare. He wore boots and a sword and a ragged length of homespun weave tied around his hips that covered him to his knees, for it had been a cursed hot day.

And he had not much respect for royal princesses, but he had a little respect for the number of mounted soldiers who'd preceded her.

Though perhaps only very little.

"Forgive me, princess. What bare part of me offends you most? I will cover it now."

"Your chest."

With a nod, Aruk began to untie the knot at his hip.

A frown creased her brow. "What are you doing?"

"I have only enough cloth to cover my bottom or my top, your highness. But as it is my chest that most offends you, I hope you'll forgive me when I flaunt my cock."

Her mouth dropped open. And a very pretty mouth it was. Pretty enough that the cock he was soon to flaunt began to stir.

Or perhaps what stirred him was not her mouth at all, but what came out of it. For her eyes narrowed and she said, "I will give you a small napkin to cover it, too."

Aruk laughed. "I would be grateful, your highness."

The crowd murmured and jostled again as she gracefully dismounted. She wore a gossamer cape over a dress of white silk, and she unfastened that cape's golden clips as she approached.

Though not near to Aruk's height, she was a tall woman, with the top of her head on level with his chin. A soft perfume reached him, a scent both sharp as a lemon and sweet as its blossom.

She crooked her finger, and obediently he bent his head. That scent spun around him as she draped the cape over his left shoulder, and the warmth of her fingers as she smoothed it into place crosswise over his chest filled his cock with answering heat.

Clipping the cape closed beneath his right arm, she placed her palm against his ribs and softly said, "Keep this glowing mark on your skin concealed, or you will find yourself in chains."

The ward that protected him from spells. Most people from these realms did not even recognize what it was. "Why?"

She gave him no reason, but pressed a heavy coin into his palm. "With this you may purchase swift passage upon any ship you choose. Leave this kingdom as quickly as you can. All from the Dead Lands must stay away."

"Why?" he asked again.

She looked to him in exasperation, as if unused to being questioned. "Perhaps because you are conquerers and butcherers who kill kings and steal thrones."

"Only from tyrants. Is that what you fear—that I'll steal your throne? Be not a tyrant, then."

Dryly she said, "I only fear that you'll inspire others to tear off their clothes."

He grinned. "I should like to inspire that in you, princess."

Her lips quirked slightly, but she only stepped back and swiftly mounted her horse. "Let me never see you again, warrior."

"You will not," he told her—for it was likely true. His duty and blood obligation had demanded that he sail away from here long before she made the same demand. And a long journey lay ahead. No thought did he have of returning.

Without looking back, she rode away from him, continuing her parade down the street. Easy then it should have been to leave. But he watched until she was out of sight.

Then Aruk did what his duty demanded. As dark clouds gathered over the Illwind Sea, he sailed away from Savadon.

And two days later, he was lost to the waves.

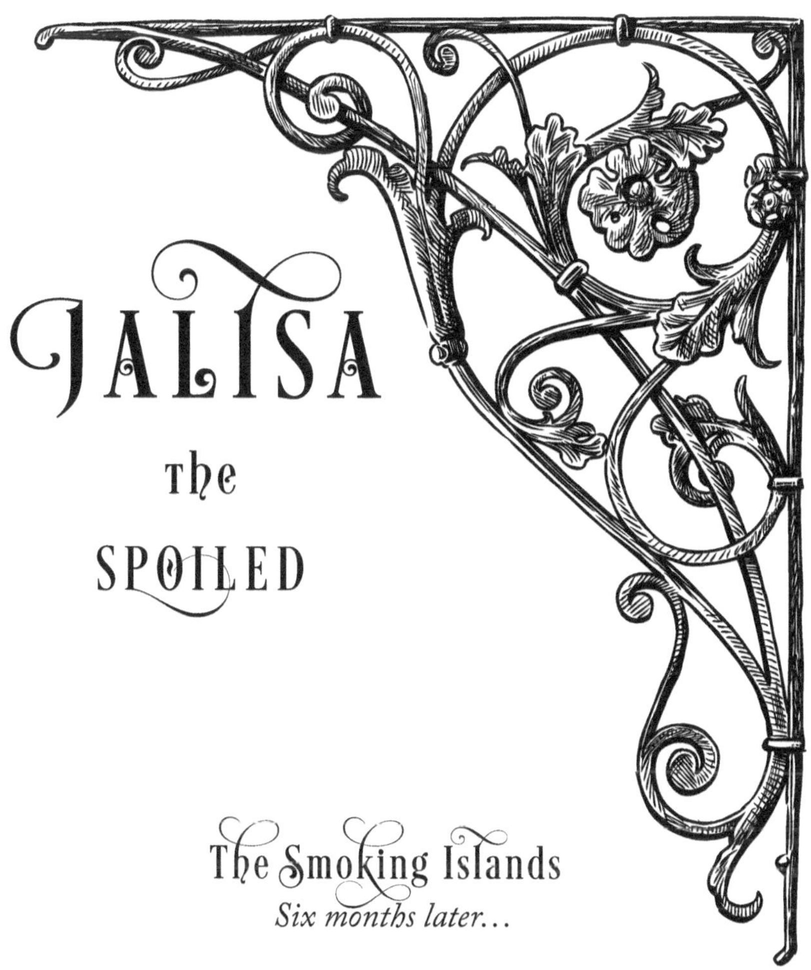

Jalisa
the
Spoiled

The Smoking Islands
Six months later…

Salt water splashed into Jalisa's mouth as she fell yet again, struggling to drag the dinghy onto the sand. A small wave broke behind the stern and assisted her next heave, and when the water receded the boat did not go with it. She collapsed onto the beach and breathlessly laughed, exhausted and sunburned and *free*.

She would only be free for a short time. Yet even temporary freedom was so sweet.

Climbing to her feet, she secured the dinghy's rope around the trunk of a palm tree, then looked out to where her ship was anchored beyond the mouth of the cove. Not a breeze stirred through the canvas sails—nor would it, until she returned.

Turning away from the water, she trudged through the soft, shifting sands. Only dawn it was, so the sun had not yet warmed the beach to burn her feet. Water dripped down her bare legs. She had abandoned her long, tangling skirts her first day upon the sea. The sleeveless silk shift she wore now had soaked through, and she might as well have been naked. Her hair was in a salty, ratty tangle. Her lips were chapped and nose peeling. And the finest part of it all was that there was no one to see, no one to care that Jalisa wasn't the pretty princess she was supposed to be.

Soon she would have to make herself into a pretty bride. But not yet.

She consulted the map of the island that her handmaid's brother, Bashir, had sketched into parchment almost a year past. A volcanic peak towered ahead, the steep sides covered in lush vegetation. The hut that stored all of her provisions lay at the western end of this cove, at the base of that mountain.

In no other way could she have stocked away so many supplies without being found out, except to have almost nothing to do with the process. As her coming of age day neared, Bashir had stored enough dried food to last a voyage to the western shore. Then for six months, it had waited here for her, because her father had not tried to marry her off as quickly as she'd expected him to.

Then two months ago, Prince Wanieer had arrived, as odious as could be. Almost as odious as her father's advisor, Fin Ketles, whose leering attentions had begun with the first budding of her breasts. So it became time to flee. Marriage still awaited her, but at least it would be a husband of her choosing.

The hut stood precisely where the map claimed it would be. After six months of neglect—and particularly since a savage storm had blown across the Illwind Sea a few days after she'd come of age—she had expected more disrepair. The thatched roof caved in, perhaps. Or a wall blown down, the door hanging open. She had prepared herself to find at least some of her goods spoiled by moisture or rummaged through by animals, yet the hut appeared intact.

A simple wooden latch secured the door. Swinging it open, she stepped into the dim interior—and froze as her senses registered the presence she'd not heard from outside.

A man. Lying upon a woven mat, his heavy muscles covered with a gossamer cloth. The golden glow of a ward carved into his ribs shone through the shee. And she could not mistake the rough pumping movement of his big fist, or the jutting length that made a tent of the filmy covering.

"*Jalisa.*" That deep groan sent her gaze flying to his face, but his eyes were closed, his teeth clenched. "I love how you spread those pretty thighs so wide for me. So eager you are for my cock."

Never had she been eager for any cock. Never had she spread her thighs for anyone.

And never had she heard anyone say her name with such naked want, unfettered by calculation and ambition and greed.

Faster he jerked his thick curving length. His hips arched up from the mat, the gossamer slipping away. "Your cunt…so tight…fill you up, princess, *so deep.*"

Skin prickling with heat, she watched him bring a gold coin to his mouth and press it to his lips. That firm mouth she knew. That glowing rune she knew. She knew that long black hair and the cheekbones like blades.

The barbarian from the parade.

"Jalisa." Head back, the cords in his neck stood in sharp relief. "Give your sweet mouth to me as I— *Unnnnnh.*"

Now he kissed a coin imprinted with her likeness as he grunted and shook, pounding his shaft into his fist before abruptly stilling, ropes of seed splashing across his ridged abdomen.

Chest heaving, he eased his muscular ass down to the mat again. He lay the coin over his heart before rolling his head toward the door in languid motion, as if utterly pleased and spent. He blinked, then regarded her without much reaction while she stared at him, mouth hanging open, every inch of her skin hot and tight and tingling.

"This is the finest dream yet," he said gruffly, his hungry gaze consuming her from head to toe.

Jalisa closed her gaping mouth. Then opened it again. But…what was there to say?

Except, "Again you are bare, warrior."

A slow smile curved his firm mouth. "So are you, princess. And more beautiful than ever I imagined."

For she left nothing to his imagination, standing before him in a transparent shift, with nipples hardened and cunt slick. Because he had just… With her name on his lips.

And the *coin*.

Silently she backed out of the hut and closed the door. So hard it was to think. Monkeys screeched in the trees. A multitude of birds seemed to be chirping and singing and flapping around inside her brain.

Had she gone mad? Was this a long-delayed scaling of a magic spell—an unraveled hangman's rope becoming a knotted mind? Or was it the effect of a fever? Was she perhaps still in her bed, drowning in her own lungs?

It couldn't be. Even vomiting, never in the palace had she been so…unkempt.

Through the door, she called out, "Why are you on my island, warrior?"

It opened. So tall he was, ducking his head to leave the hut. Around his hips he tied a fraying rag barely long enough to cover what she now knew hung between his legs. A small napkin would not have sufficed.

Oh, and so thick and hard his thighs were. And his chest. And his arms.

And his head. "This is *your* island?" he asked.

"Would I be here if it was not?"

He shrugged his massive shoulders. "It is not my island and yet I am here."

"All of the Smoking Islands belong to Savadon—which you were supposed to leave and never return. Why are you here?"

He narrowed his eyes as if the answer required deep thought, idly scratching his chest. "A wave swept me from my ship and into the sea."

Oh. "Then you swam here?"

"Only part of the way. I grabbed hold of a kindly dolphin's fin and rode upon its back for a few days. But a monster squid attacked the dolphin's pod, and I only narrowly escaped after cutting through one of its arms. Then the sharks came, but I had lost my sword battling the squid, and so a full night I spent heroically battering them to death with my fists before I could swim the remaining distance."

May the gods have mercy upon him. The solitude had addled his brain. "How long have you been here alone, warrior?"

"Since two days past your parade."

It was *that* storm he'd been swept to sea in? Six months he had been here, then.

Her heart stilled. "Did you eat all of my provisions?"

"Those were also yours?"

"*Were?*"

He grinned. "Still some are left. I touched none of the

prunes. Far better fruits are found in the trees. And I am a mighty hunter. If you fear starving here, you need not."

"I do not intend to *be* here."

His gaze sharpened. "You are not also marooned?"

"Of course not. I do not ride dolphins to islands. I have a ship."

Sheer relief filled his expression. "Then I will leave with you."

"And starve upon the sea? How are we to survive a three month voyage to the western shore when you have eaten all the provisions?" Sheer frustration burst from her in a sharp screech. "You thieving pig! If you are such a mighty hunter, could you not have hunted your meals instead of raiding my stores?"

Unbothered he seemed. "So I will hunt and fill them again. Where on the western shore do you go?"

"Grimhold." She kicked sullenly at the sand, because it was true—the island might provide what she needed. But so *long* the preparations would take. "Kael the Conqueror seeks a bride."

So utterly still the barbarian became. His voice deepened as he asked, "And you intend that bride to be you?"

"I do."

"Did you not disapprove of barbarians from the Dead Lands who killed tyrants and stole their thrones?"

"That is why I would marry him. So he might come and kill a tyrant."

"Who? Solegius of Aremond?"

Who needed killing, too. But—"I hoped he would start with my father."

He gave her a doubtful look. "A tyrant he is?"

Throat tight, Jalisa nodded.

"Because he does he not buy you enough silks? Or because he forces you to marry?"

As if she were a silly girl. Fire burned in her gut and she pivoted away from him. "I think instead I will send a ship back for you, warrior."

The maddening barbarian kept pace with her through the sand. "He is no Solegius of Aremond, murdering and enslaving all those who stand against him."

"Not for lack of trying."

"What do you mean by that?"

"He does not fill his mines with slaves, true, but he has enslaved some in other ways. And he orders all who stand against him executed. But the fates conspire against him, because the methods he uses keep failing. And in Savadon, if a hangman's rope breaks or if an executioner's axe shatters, the law states they must be sent into exile, instead."

"Is this what has happened to you—exile? Did you stand against him?"

"No." Not openly. Not for a long time. "I decided to find someone who might more successfully stand against him."

"I will do it."

"I would rather the Conqueror, for I know he killed four tyrant kings with great success."

"Kael is already married."

She stopped dead in her tracks. "Are you certain?"

"I am. My brother and I were hired to bolster the army at the southern pass of Grimhold before we came to Savadon by way of Aremond." Intensely he regarded her with unreadable expression. "He married a princess from Ivermere."

Everything within Jalisa deflated—then filled again. *Hired to bolster the army.* "You are a hired sword?"

"I am." He gave a wry smile. "Though my sword is at the bottom of the sea."

She would buy him a new one. "What is your fee?"

For a long time his dark gaze searched her face, her eyes. Finally he said in a gruff voice, "One night in your bed."

In astonishment she stared at him. "You want a night in my bed? And that is all?"

Jaw clenched, he gave a single nod.

"Very well. If that is all it will cost me, then we have a deal." She laughed. "You sell your services so cheaply, warrior."

His face darkened. "Cheaply?"

"I was willing to marry Kael the Conqueror in exchange for what you offer to me at only the price of my virginity. My whole life I would have spent married to a man I didn't love, with no other purpose but giving birth to his heirs. You could have asked to marry me, and for me to make you a king, and I would have agreed. Are you certain you do not want that? I do not want you to feel cheated. Especially as this job carries deep risk."

The skin over his cheekbones drew taut. Hoarsely he said, "I cannot have a wife or a kingdom. When this task is finished, duty calls me elsewhere."

"Ah." Duty, she understood all too well. "I would not take advantage of you, warrior. What of a mountain of gold? Will you not ask for that?"

"I cannot carry a mountain of gold upon a horse."

"I suppose you cannot. So one night it is, then. And in exchange, you hand to me true freedom." She sighed happily, her chest swelling with emotion. Because if this warrior succeeded, then her freedom would not be temporary. "And it is so much less than I ever expected to pay. Less than I have already paid. So yes, warrior—I think you sell your services *very* cheaply."

ARUK
the
FOOL

The Illwind Sea

WHAT THE PRINCESS CALLED CHEAP MIGHT COME AT the cost of Aruk's heart. A fool he was. Such a fool. The woman he'd woven so many dreams around did not exist. She had been but a focus for his mind as the endless days passed on the island, burning with frustration that he was trapped in the middle of the Illwind Sea instead of helping his brother fulfill their sacred obligation.

His brother still lived, at least. Even when separated, Aruk could feel the distant presence of his twin like a touch at the back of his head. So he had no fear that whatever obstacles Strax faced upon that tournament route had defeated him.

But he hated that his brother had faced them alone. For no doubt Mara would have nothing to do with him.

What would Strax have given for a single night with her? Aruk suspected that his brother would have given anything. A fine woman she was.

Not a haughty, spoiled princess who demanded that Aruk cover himself, then threatened to put him in chains for exposing a harmless rune, then screeched at him for eating unmarked provisions that had seemed abandoned and left for the very purpose he'd used them: to nourish someone trapped on the island. And now she wanted him to kill a king whom Aruk suspected had done nothing better or worse than any other king. Every ruler punished those who rebelled against him. And these had only known exile? That was not what Aruk called a tyrant.

More probably, this princess rebelled because the husband chosen for her wasn't to her liking.

And because Aruk was a fool, every part of his heart rebelled at the thought of her taking *any* husband.

He had not meant to think of her for even a single moment after the parade. She had stirred his cock, true. Because she had smelled so fine, and her mouth was so lush, and her tongue so sharp. The imperious way she looked down at him had fired his blood. And so his first imaginings had been of the princess beneath him, instead. Not haughty and demanding but writhing and begging.

So very satisfying those imaginings had been. And

that should have been the end of them. But although he'd tried, no other woman could he picture while stroking his cock. Until he never even *tried* to think of other women. His mind had returned to her again and again. So often that it almost seemed as if she had been his companion on this island these past six months.

But the woman he'd conjured in his mind had not screeched. She'd not been spoiled. A sharp tongue she'd still had—but also a warm and generous heart.

The woman he'd conjured would not murder a king or buy a kingdom for the cost of her virginity.

But that was not a price Aruk would truly demand. No night with this princess would he have. For he had no intention of killing her father. Only of escaping this island.

In all his dreams of Jalisa, never had he imagined that it would be she who rescued him. But it was for the best, if time spent with the princess could cure this obsession that ailed him. For even as she'd screeched, his cock and his heart had ached with need for her. As she'd dangled marriage and a lifetime in front of him, so badly he'd wanted to take them.

Yet she seemed quite pleased that he didn't.

No time had they wasted before leaving. Only two days' voyage it was back to Savadon, so no need to stock more provisions. Aruk studied her now as he rowed the dinghy to the sailing ship anchored outside the shallow cove. The princess looked as if she might have truly spent six months on an island with him. Sun and wind had pinkened her pale skin. Her hair was a wild tangle. Eyes closed, she sat in the boat with her face lifted to the rising sun, a soft smile on her lips.

"What did you mean when you said I offer you true freedom?"

That smile widened, as if simply the thought brought her renewed joy. "Only that I would not have to be what was intended for me. Instead I will be what I choose to be."

"You do not wish to be a queen?"

"A queen? That would mean nothing in my father's kingdom." Now she looked at him, her gaze so direct. "Never would I rule after my father died. The husband my father chose for me would. The only purpose intended for me is to breed heirs."

"Is that not a queen's duty? You do not want children?"

"I want children when I am ready to have children. Not because a husband is ready to get heirs upon me. So I would like to be queen, warrior. What I do not want is to be a bride, whose only purpose is in marriage and breeding and looking pretty."

"You do not wish to marry?" No husband then would Aruk have to hate.

Or kill.

She shrugged. "Not if it means always bowing to the wishes of a husband or marrying a man who wants the throne more than he wants me. So perhaps I will not marry at all. Perhaps a string of lovers I will take."

Lovers? Aruk couldn't stop his snarl. His hard pull

on the oars sent her swaying backward and forward as she laughed at him.

"You disapprove, warrior? After demanding to be the first of them?"

She was right to laugh. It was a fool's reaction. Yet jealousy filled his gut and Aruk wanted to demand that he would be her first and her last and her only.

And he would not even be her first. Still he said to her, "You are a virgin. Do you truly know what you agreed to, and what I will do to you?"

"Of course. You will spread my thighs and shove your cock into me and then rut until you spend. Though I hope you will not spend inside me."

Spilling his seed deep within the hot, wet clasp of her. His shaft stiffened at the mere thought.

Yet that could only be fantasy. "Never would I spend inside a woman who was not my wife." A woman he could not stay with, if he got her with child.

"Then we are agreed."

"I do not think we are." Except in the broadest of details. He hauled back on the oars. "Your legs I would spread. Then I would settle my head between them and feast on your cunt until sweet honey dripped down your thighs."

Her breath caught. Lips parted, she stared at him.

Another stroke of the oars. His firm grip on them was all that prevented Aruk from reaching for her. "And when you are wet and soft and swollen with your need, then I will sink my cock into you. Again and again. Full deep, never stopping until I feel the hot squeeze of your cunt as you come."

Her fingers rolled into fists against her thighs. The shift she wore had dried, no longer transparent, yet still he could clearly see the hardness of her nipples.

"Why would you?" she whispered.

"Why would I fuck you? It is the fee." One he would never collect. Though he'd begun to wish her father was a tyrant in truth.

"Why make me come? Why care whether I enjoy it at all?"

He frowned. "What sort of man would not care?"

"I think most only care for their own pleasure."

The sort of men she knew were not men at all, then. "That *is* my pleasure. Not the hot clasp of your cunt around my cock, sweet though it would be. Pleasure is knowing I made you scream and writhe as I fucked you with it."

As she squirmed now upon the seat in the boat. As if trying to ease an ache within her.

As if she were already dripping with honey.

Though he'd spent by his own hand less than an hour ago, hot and throbbing his cock was now, knowing that she had imagined what he'd described and her need slickened her cunt.

Breathing harsh, he swung the oars forward out of the water, securing them within the boat. "Give to me a taste."

Confusion lined her brow. "A taste?"

"Of your cunt. Now." A night he would not have. But

he would have this.

Her eyes narrowed. "My father is not yet dead."

"And you would not like me to feel cheated by the cheap price I set. What if the taste of you is not what I dreamed? Best I be certain now."

She bit her lip as if against a laugh. But not only amusement did he see. Temptation was there, too.

"Come stand before me, Jalisa. When I make you come on my tongue, you can also be certain that what I said is how it will be."

Indecision only warred over her beautiful face for another second. Then she rose, the boat rocking from side to side in the water. He held out his hand to steady her. The trusting curl of her fingers around his also curled around his heart in a tighter grip.

So fucked he was.

"Step up here on the seat," he said, voice raw with hunger. With her feet in the bottom of the boat, she was at an awkward angle to his mouth. Yet if she stood on the bench where he sat, a perfect height she would be.

She stepped up between his thighs, gripping his shoulder when the dinghy rocked again. "It wobbles."

"I will hold you steady," he vowed, and so he did, taking her hips in a firm grip as she rose before him.

Again she looked down at him, though not imperiously. Instead he only saw nervousness and curiosity and arousal. And the deliberately haughty tone she put into her voice as she said, "You may taste me now, warrior," only made him grin.

As did the realization of why she called him 'warrior.' "Do you not wish to know the name of the man who is feasting on your cunt?"

She blinked, as if that had not occurred to her. Then she gave him a considering look. "I don't think so, no."

Yet the way she flattened her lips together, as if repressing a smile, and the dimple that suddenly appeared in her cheek said that she only teased him.

He could tease, too. "Pull up your shift."

Immediately her lips softened and parted. Her breathing deepened. With fingers at her hips, she ruched the silk upward, baring her upper thighs an inch at a time, then the cleft between. Standing as she was, her thighs pressed together, he saw nothing of her deeper cunt. Only the slit at the front that nestled her pretty clit—but that was all he needed to make her come.

Already she glistened with her need—and she was completely bare. "Is this a princess's cunt? They pamper and groom you even here?"

"No," she said softly. "I was being prepared for marriage."

For another man to look upon her. But she was *his*.

She gave a soft cry of surprise as he abruptly dragged her forward, and his mouth opened against her, his tongue slicking into that little slit. He groaned in pleasure at the first taste of her wetness. Salty she was from the sea, yet her flavor beneath was so sweet and heady.

Her body trembled violently as, with broad strokes

of his tongue, Aruk teased her clit before sucking that pretty bud between his lips. A guttural sound she made, curling forward and releasing her grip on the silk to grab fistfuls of his hair.

"Warrior," she gasped. "Warrior."

With a growl low in his throat, he tore his ravenous mouth from her cunt and angled his head back to look up at her. She was flushed, panting, her hair hanging around her face.

"Oh, do not stop." With urgent hands, she tried to shove his head back down. "Do not stop."

Unmoved, Aruk only waited, her sweetness on his tongue and lips, hungry for her cunt but hungrier still for something else.

She gave him a sudden dour look and tugged at his hair. "Then what do I call you, *warrior*?"

He grinned. "Aruk."

"Aruk," she repeated softly, and the fingers of her right hand let go of his hair to trace a path along his jaw. "So sweet a night with you will be."

Fierce ache gripped his heart. Roughly he dragged her to his mouth again. This, the only taste he would have. So much better it was than his imaginings, with her fingernails digging into his scalp and the helpless rocking of her hips against his face. Her knees gave out and he held her up, sucking and licking her clit, his fingers digging into the soft cheeks of her ass. More frantic her movements became. His name she said, again and again, her voice high with frantic wonder. Then she stilled all at once, her soft flesh convulsing against his tongue, her teeth clenched on a scream.

Tremors slipped through her as he sucked on her clit again, and she pushed at his head. "Stop," she panted. "Please stop."

Too sensitive now. So no more would Aruk have, unless he hurt her.

Never would he do that.

With a last deep inhalation of her scent, he drew back, letting the silk fall into place to cover her. A fool he was to have done this. For he had told himself there were some things he would *not* do to spend a night in her arms—such as kill a king who did not deserve killing.

Yet now, after this taste of her…Aruk could think of almost nothing that he wouldn't do for another lick. And that a mere taste. To have her for one sweet night? To fuck her so deep and hard and feel her cling to him, calling his name?

He might do anything.

JALISA

the

SELFISH

The Illwind Sea

JALISA WAS STILL TREMBLING FROM THE PLEASURE OF Aruk's mouth when they reached her ship. This freedom she had now was so fine, indeed. For when she was the princess her father wanted her to be, never could she have followed her desire and let a warrior lick her cunt. And so wonderful it had been. He'd been so hungry for her—and never had the pleasure of her own touch approached the ecstasy of his.

Oh, how incredible it would be when she could always follow her own desire, without regard for what anyone else wanted her to do. Especially if she desired a man such as Aruk.

He looked up alongside the ship, frowning. "Where is your crew?"

"I have no crew."

"A ship of this size must have a crew."

She shook her head. "This ship is spelled to always sail on the finest winds, wherever I want it to go."

Darkly he scowled. "That is no simple spell. And dangerous."

So it was. "I paid a great deal for it."

"What of the scaling? How did you ward against it for a boat of this size?"

Because a spell always had a consequence. If a spell healed, it was by stealing health from somewhere else. If it strengthened, it was by stealing strength from somewhere else. And never could the scaling of those spells be predicted, whether the consequence was large or small. Healing a broken bone might only scale and leave a bruise on someone else—someone who was unprotected from the scaling, which might be anyone who didn't wield magic—or it might break that person in half.

"For fair winds," Aruk continued, "somewhere else will receive foul winds. When was this ship spelled? Six months past?"

"You think it caused the storm that swept you here?" Jalisa shook her head. "Sometimes, warrior, the weather is just the weather. And it was two months past that the ship was spelled."

He did not like it. That she could see. But she had not tossed magic about carelessly. She would not risk such a scaling to harm innocents, either.

A better sailor Aruk was than she, more familiar with boats, for he didn't fumble with the ropes and pulleys that secured the dinghy. His arms bulged with corded muscle as he hauled the small boat into place alongside the rail. They climbed to the main deck, treading across the weathered gray boards.

He looked around them doubtfully. "You meant to sail three months on this wreck?"

She could not have bought a yacht without her father knowing. So it was a fisherman's ship, old but sturdy. "It is seaworthy."

"Barely." He tapped a knuckle against the mast as if to check it for dry rot. "Who made the spell for you?"

So he was not off of that yet? He seemed more bothered by knowing this spell had been cast then when she'd described what her father was.

"A witch of the Dead Lands."

His eyes widened, then narrowed. "What do you know of witches?"

More than anyone else in Savadon, for witches were not commonly in these western realms. Almost everyone born in the Dead Lands was born with great ability to cast spells and magic within them. As Aruk had been. That glowing symbol on his side was proof of the magic in him.

Yet those from the Dead Lands also believed that

the magic slowly pushed the world out of balance until there was a disastrous Reckoning. And so most bound their magic to their skin with a small rune, and they deliberately never learned the spoken spells that would bend the world to their will.

Yet some still did. The witches, who were all highly respected within the Dead Lands. For they did not bind their magic, and they knew spells, yet only in the most dire of circumstances would use them—such as a child dying of infection or sickness, or the most fatal of injuries. Because most injuries would heal. They simply took time and patience and left a scar.

Outside of the Dead Lands, spells were used more carelessly. Healers were common even for the most minor of pains. But because the scaling could not be known, healers always resided in warded chambers or huts, so the consequences of the magic could not escape and harm an innocent person. And within that hut, the healer would keep small animals such as mice or insects for the scaling to target.

Yet a ship could not fit in a warded chamber. So Aruk believed that an innocent must have been affected by the scaling.

"A witch would never cast a spell on a ship like this," he said.

That was true. But still, a witch was the reason Jalisa had known the spell. But she thought this warrior might disapprove of how she'd cast it even more vehemently than he disapproved of the spell already.

"Do you think kindness and love would keep it afloat?" she teased him. For those were the magics that had no scaling. Pure they were, working change not by stealing from elsewhere, but by adding themselves to the world, like a low flame beneath a pot of water, slowly warming it.

Though in truth...kindness and love *would* keep this boat afloat. Because this spell had not been of pure magic, but everything Jalisa had been taught of magic was born from love.

As if she thought he mocked him with mention of true magic and love, Aruk cast her a dark look, shaking his head. "How do we sail?"

"With but a thought from its captain." Which she gave now. The breeze suddenly picked up, filling the sails. The creaking ship began to slide across the water.

And though he disliked the magic behind it, the spell was done. No more fine winds would be stolen to create it.

"You should take the ship!" she called over the new sound of rushing water against the bow. "When my father is dead and your duty calls you away!"

For that is what Aruk had said—he could not marry because of duty. And his voyage had been interrupted, so after his job for her was done, he would sail away again.

Now the thought of his leaving filled her chest with a tight ache. "Will you ever return to Savadun, warrior?"

He grunted, jaw tight. "You told me that I should not."

"It would not be so dangerous with my father dead."

She grinned at him, fluttering her lashes. "And if you please me in my bed the first night, perhaps I would take you again."

So fierce and determined his expression became. "I would please you so well that you will abandon your plan to take many others to your bed."

"Well, I would not take them all at once!" she teased. "Or perhaps I would. When I am queen, who is to tell me how to behave?"

A muscle worked in his jaw. "Will you be a selfish queen, then, demanding men to warm your bed—so that I might have to return to you for different reason?"

To kill another tyrant, as her father was. Hurt speared through her then. He spoke as if she would take lovers without regard for whether they wanted her or not. As if she would order them to her bed instead of only seeking the same pleasure that he'd given by wanting her so much.

Tightly she said, "If what I do harms no one, what issue do you have?"

"You think those you take to your bed will not fall in love with you and be destroyed when you are done with them? That is no harm?"

She laughed, though beneath it lay pain, sharpening. "Is that all it takes to fall in love? Are you not in danger, then, for asking to spend a night with me? Suddenly the fee you wanted seems not so insignificant or so cheap. I did not know one night would earn me your heart."

Though they both knew it would not. So she did not

know why he suddenly disapproved of her hope that she would find love and pleasure in someone's arms. For he was not staying to give it.

"You are welcome to the ship," she said tautly when he gave no immediate response. "We will add it to your fee. What duty did you say calls you away?"

"Aremond's tournament," he said, voice harsh.

She knew of that tournament. Dozens of warriors had passed through Savadon on their way to seek some relic in the realms north of the Illwind Sea. Whoever brought the relic back to Aremond won the tournament's prize—a pile of gold.

The pile of gold that Aruk had refused from her. And he was so far behind the others, he must have already lost. Unless he meant to ambush and steal the relic from the victor as they made their way back to Aremond.

"And is that what you will do? Return to that tournament route?"

He nodded. "It is."

Her heart constricted. And she understood him not at all. "Did you not say—"

The bow tipped up suddenly, throwing her back. Aruk's strong arms caught her.

"What was that?" The sails were still full, yet the boat had stopped. "Did we hit a rock?"

Which should not have happened. The spell made this ship always sail true.

"I do not think so," Aruk said slowly, eyes fixed ahead.

"You ought to have spelled this ship against sea monsters, too."

Jalisa gasped in horror. A huge gray tentacle was coiling around the bow. Enormous it was, slick and pulsating, the suckers hungrily seeking.

A monster squid. Which could tear apart ships, so the vessels spilled out contents and passengers, and the squid could feast at will. Frantically she looked to the stern, where another tentacle had begun winding over the deck.

Not a hint of fear did she hear in Aruk's voice when it rumbled in her ear. "Do you have any weapons aboard?"

"No."

"What did you intend to do if you came across pirates?"

"Not fight them! I would make the ship outrun them."

But already that option was too late. The winds blew, but even spelled winds could not free a ship from the grip of a monster squid.

Aruk led her to the ship's mast. "Hold tight to this," he told her. "I must kill the monster before those tentacles rip apart the timbers."

"Kill it with what?"

From the small bundle he'd brought from the island, he showed her a palm-sized stone with a sharp edge. "This razor I made."

"Do you mean to give the monster a shave with that little blade?"

His teeth flashed in a broad grin. "It sliced into my face often enough, so it will likely also slice into a squid's.

Hold fast to that mast until I return."

With smooth stride, he moved to the edge of the deck and leapt up onto the gunwale as if his thick muscles were made of springs. He looked down into the water, and a hearty laugh broke from him.

"It is my old friend! Perhaps he has waited for me all this time—but this day, I will not stop after cutting off only one arm. It is this monster's day to die!"

And with stone blade clenched between his teeth, Aruk dove in.

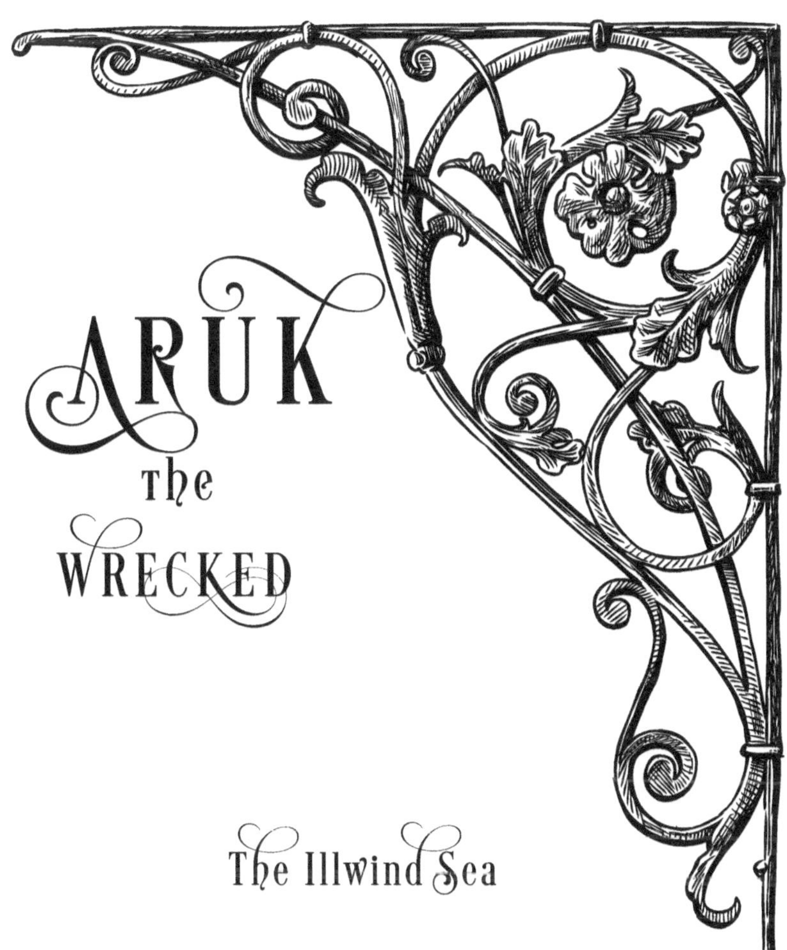

ARUK the WRECKED

The Illwind Sea

Aruk had heard that monster squids had memories as long as their arms. True that seemed now, for apparently the squid had left the deep sea to lay in wait for him near the island. He knew not if the squid intended vengeance for the lost arm, but whatever feud between them lay in that foul brain, Aruk would end it today.

Under the water was a slithering mass of tentacles. A firm grip on the ship it had—and the vessel was already lost, Aruk saw. Timbers beneath the waterline had splintered and cracked. No spell for fair winds would prevent water from filling the hold and sinking them to the bottom of the sea.

He surfaced again. His disobedient princess stood not at the mast but clinging to the rail, her wide-eyed terror melting into relief when she saw him. "Throw everything into the dinghy and drop it free of the ship!" he called to her.

"I will!" She spun and disappeared from his sight.

With a screech of wood, the ship splintered in half, the center popping upward, the bow and stern tipping downward into the water. Cursing, Aruk dove under, stone knife in hand.

Broken planks rained down through the water, sharpened edges like wooden daggers. Feet kicking, Aruk arrowed through the water to the center mass of those tentacles. All the arms were wrapped around the ship—and so the squid's great eye was unprotected.

As he dove toward it, his own face he saw reflected in that black orb, a mask of rage and purpose. He plunged the stone blade into the fleshy eye. Blood spilled out like ink, blinding him with black clouds. The squid began to thrash, convulsing tentacles still wrapped around the ends of the ship, tearing apart the two ends and flinging them about.

And Jalisa was still aboard.

Aruk's heart pounded with sudden fear, his lungs were afire, but the squid was not dead yet. Deeper he shoved his arm, hacking into the monster's brain.

All went still.

Aruk jerked his arm free and kicked for the surface. He broke through on a great heaving gasp for air, and in the next breath shouted, "Jalisa!"

The ship was scattered over gentle waves. He struck for the dinghy, swimming fast. Gripping the side, he heaved himself up and looked into the small boat. She had managed to toss his bundle into the bottom but no more.

"Jalisa!"

His frantic gaze scanned the wreckage. There she was—clinging to a floating plank. Unmoving, facedown. Crimson blood soaked her silk shift.

No. Painful dread split through his chest. He raced through the water, diving beneath wreckage too big to push aside. At her side he surfaced, praying to all the gods as he gently lifted her head from the plank to see her face.

She still breathed. His heart began beating again, then stopped as he saw her injury. A splintered piece of wood the length of a short sword had pierced her side.

He had once been stabbed in the same place. It was not a fatal wound. But it would be if he did not get her out of the water.

Cradling her still form against his chest, backward he swam toward the dinghy. He was almost to that small boat when the first dorsal fin sliced through the water nearby. Drawn by the squid's blood.

Drawn by Jalisa's blood.

The sharks were big enough to tip over their small boat. If a frenzy began, she would not be safe.

Kissing her soft lips, Aruk carefully lifted her into the dinghy.

Then into the water he went again. With his knife, he made a shallow slice across his thigh. A full night this had taken before, and he had not that much time. Better to draw them quickly and get this over with.

The first shark attacked from beneath, a swift nightmare of gaping jaws and dagger teeth. With a mighty swing of his arm, Aruk battered his fist into its head.

By the time the shark's gray body settled dead onto the sea floor, he'd sent eight more sinking to join it. When no more fins were in sight, Aruk climbed into the boat. For the briefest moment, Jalisa opened her eyes.

Alive. But so pale she was. And still she bled.

He would *not* lose her. Had he known a spell, his own life he would have given to save her. But no magic did he have but the emotion in his heart—and the untiring strength that emotion gave to his arms.

Eyes blazing with it, he struck the oars into the water and began to row.

Jalisa the Difficult

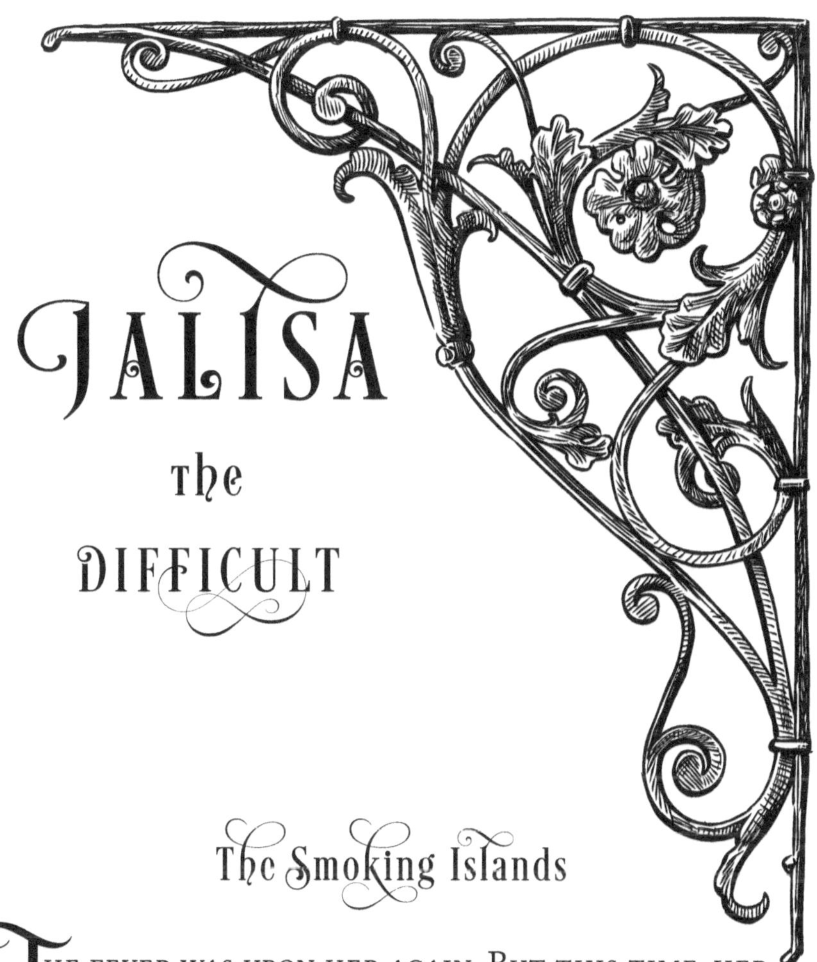

The Smoking Islands

THE FEVER WAS UPON HER AGAIN. BUT THIS TIME, HER lungs did not seem to be drowning. Somewhere nearby, monkeys screeched. A woven mat she felt beneath her back, featherlight gossamer blanketing her front.

Restlessly she moved. "Aruk?"

"Shh, princess." A soft rumble his voice was, and cool water touched her lips. "Be at ease."

Her throat and tongue were parched. She drank thirstily, then whimpered softly when he drew the water away.

"Slowly."

Or she would vomit it all up. She nodded and the

movement made her head swim. Her voice seemed a cross between a whisper and a croak. "I still do not believe there were kindly dolphins."

She heard his quiet laugh, but when Jalisa's own weak laugh shook her body, pain ripped through her side.

"Be at ease," he said softly again. "I stitched your wound as I would a battlefield injury. But it will hurt for some time."

And she was fevered, so still in danger. With strength born of desperation, she caught his wrist. Her eyes would not properly focus in the dim hut, and he was but a giant shadow looming beside her.

"If I die," she croaked, "even though you would not have your night with me, please kill my father anyway. Or all of Savadon will be as Aremond is, and ruled by a sorcerer tyrant."

"Your father is a sorcerer?" was his grim reply.

"No." Such effort that short answer was, yet more effort she had to make. "But magic he always seeks for his own corrupt gain. Please. If I am dead, no one will hold him in check."

"You will *not* die, princess." Strong hands cradled her hot cheeks. His voice was hoarse as he vowed, "Never will I let you."

And that seemed to be the only promise Aruk would make to her. But no more effort could she give.

Her fingers fell away from his wrist, and she knew no more.

* * *

ARUK'S PROMISE HE KEPT, AND she did not die. Jalisa knew not how many days he tended to her fever, but his gentle care continued after it broke. With every movement, the pain from the wound in her side jabbed deep and stole her breath—and so Aruk assisted her every move, attended to every need that she had. No embarrassment could she feel, even during the intimate tasks. Too grateful she was. Yet still it was a relief when enough of her strength returned for Jalisa to manage those tasks on her own.

And still he cared for her. When she finally could stand and walk, merely crossing the small hut left her weakened and shaking. So he would carry her outside, where she could enjoy the fresh breeze and warm sun, until exhaustion forced her to return to the sleeping mat.

While she had been fevered, he'd woven another mat, and every night he slept beside her. If ever she stirred in the dark, instantly he seemed to wake, asking if there was anything she needed.

All that she needed was Aruk, close beside her. So he had already given her everything.

Over the next week, she gained more strength. Except for when he hunted, Aruk carried her everywhere then, as if he feared letting her out of his sight. He had decided to make the dinghy more seaworthy, so that the small boat might carry them the two days' voyage to Savadon. Trees he felled and began to shape, explaining to her what he did and why he did it, so that she watched him not only in admiration of the way his powerful muscles gleamed beneath the sun, but in admiration of his skill and knowledge. Less strenuous tasks, such as braiding vines into ropes, he showed Jalisa how to do after she complained of being useless. So much more he showed her, too. How to start a fire with no flint and steel, how to catch and clean and roast a fish, how to make a flute from a thin hollow bone he found.

But he could not teach her to play it as beautifully as he did.

Nearly every waking hour, they spent together. Aruk told her of his twin brother, Strax, and of growing up in the wastes of the Dead Lands. Of the adventures they'd had as hired swords, the places they'd been, the things they'd done and seen.

To Jalisa, who had rarely stepped outside the palace walls and who had never been beyond the borders of Savadon, his adventures were the most wonderful of all stories.

In turn, she told him of the war-torn history of her kingdom, which served as the only route through the southern realms to the Illwind Sea, and the battles fought over the riches that the trade through Savadon brought. She told him of the heroes and villains in her own royal line, she told him of books she'd read—and said nothing at all of her own life. But if he noted how she avoided ever mentioning growing up within the palace, never did he say.

When she could trudge through the soft sand for more than a minute without having to stop to catch her breath, longer walks they took along the beach. Each day she grew stronger, and each night she fell exhausted and happy into bed, Aruk within arm's reach beside her.

And through it all, so desperately she fell in love with him.

But Jalisa knew a reckoning was coming. For he had tended to her so closely. Feeding her, bathing her.

She knew he'd seen the rune carved into her skin, a rune that matched one of his.

She knew he'd seen the small scars that climbed her inner thighs like ladders.

And she suspected the rune and the scars were why he hadn't touched her again, except to care for her in sickness. In the first weeks, her wound might have been the reason, except that more than a month had passed since the fever had broken, and her side barely pained her now. Yet still he didn't touch her. And despite the yearning ache within her, she hadn't reached out to him, either—too afraid that he would push her away.

When the reckoning came, it was not unexpected. Too quiet he'd been that morning. Together they walked along the shore, Aruk gazing out beyond the cove to where her ship had once been anchored, when he asked gruffly, "What did you pay for the wind spell?"

Painful constriction circled her heart. No use was it to lie, to name a sum of gold. Already he must know that she'd not paid with coin.

"A drowning cough," she whispered.

He drew to a halt in the sand, eyes closing. "The scaling of the spell stole the good wind from your lungs?"

Essentially that was what it had done. Almost never was the consequence exactly equal. "Yes."

"How long?"

"Almost two months." Desperately struggling for every breath, stricken by fever—all the while her father waited for her to heal, so she might be wed. "As soon as the illness passed, that was when I fled."

"Two months of drowning in your own lungs." Jaw clenched, he opened his eyes, his gaze blazing into hers. "Blood magic should *never* be used."

"Perhaps not." But it was the only magic she had.

"'Perhaps not?'" he echoed. "Do you not know *why* it should not be used?"

"Because it defeats the purpose of this rune." She passed her fingers over her hip, where the marking was—the rune that bound her magic to the border of her skin.

In the Dead Lands, that rune was a vow made to never use spells that would push the world out of balance. That was likely what it meant to him.

But that was not what the rune meant to Jalisa. She had not chosen it or made a vow. Instead it was a cage that she'd been tossed into.

And so her power was bound beneath her skin…but her blood was still full of her magic. By shedding drops of blood, she could use her magic again.

"Because it is *dangerous*," he snarled. "The scaling *always* affects the one who cast the spell. And never can anyone predict what the scaling will be. Blood magic kills the person who uses it. *Always.*"

"Eventually it will," she agreed softly. "But I won't need to use it so often after my father is dead. Until then, it is a risk I must take."

"Why must you?" he challenged fiercely, and dropped to his knees, shoving up the hem of her torn and ragged shift. Jalisa trembled as his thumb brushed over a small pink scar on her inner thigh—the most recent of the scars. "This must be the ship. But what is this one?" His fingers moved higher, touching the oldest. "What was so important that you risked your life for this?"

"My father decided to make an example of a pack of street urchins who had been stealing food from the market. They were meant to hang. I unraveled the ropes. So they were exiled, instead."

So still Aruk became. "And the scaling?"

"My hair was knotted for weeks. Which does not sound so very dire, I know," she whispered painfully. "Except that I am always supposed to be a pretty princess and my father was so very angry with me and my maids. They could not fix my hair and so he had all of theirs shaved, as criminals have their heads shaved. They had to endure that humiliation—and to me, that was the worst part of the scaling. But other scalings were not so bad. Some spells, the effect on me must have been so small that I still do not know what the scaling was."

For an endless time Aruk stared up at her, his tortured gaze searching her face. Then he glanced down again, his fingers sliding down the ladder of small scars. "All of these…?"

"To save those he would have executed for cruel and petty reasons," she said softly. "But I did not save everyone. Such as a man who beat his wife to death—no spell did I cast then."

"And the marks you hid here," he said hoarsely. "So your father would not realize what you'd done."

"Yes. And I have been mostly fortunate in the scalings. The cough was the worst."

"*Jalisa.*" He groaned her name and pressed his face into her belly, holding tight to her hips. "You should not have used it."

Her eyes burned. Did he not understand how helpless she'd been? "Then what should I have done? How could I have saved them?"

"What if the blood magic had killed you? Who would have saved them, then?" Drawing back, he looked up at her fiercely. "You *must* find another way."

"I *have*," she reminded him. "And the only blood required is my virginity."

Again his eyes closed, his face a mask of torment. "To hire my sword and kill him."

"Yes."

The one night that had seemed such a cheap price to pay…and now seemed not a price to pay at all. Instead it was the sweetest gift, that she would have one night with him before duty pulled him away.

Gently he urged her down to kneeling in the sand with him, her face on level with his. "So tell me what sort of man I am to kill."

"When I was a little girl, he was the best of men. He doted on me, spoiled me, encouraged me. Anything I wished for, he gave to me." Her breath shuddered in painful remembrance. To a young girl, such indulgence seemed like love. And she had loved him so much in return. "He was so proud of how strong my magic was. From the beginning, he made certain I had the finest tutor—a witch from the Dead Lands whom he'd rescued from slavery after she'd been stolen from her home, and her magic bound with the rune. As my father instructed her to, she taught me many spells, so that I might one day become a powerful sorcerer who could protect our people and defend our kingdom. That was the sort of man he was."

"Then he changed?" Aruk asked softly.

"He did not change," she said achingly. "All that changed was how I saw him. I was fifteen years of age when I discovered the witch was my mother—and that he'd not rescued her from slavery, but instead had purchased her from a slaver. He married her so that I would be a legitimate heir, then forced her in his bed. Then he told her that if she ever wanted to see her daughter, it could only be as my tutor. But I do not think he ever realized that she taught me more than spells—and that she taught me of true magic, too."

And that love was not just unchecked indulgence. That kindness was not just benevolent condescension. That compassion was not just prayerful pity.

She looked into Aruk's eyes. "She ruined me for what he intended—to use my power to bring other kingdoms under his heel."

"*You* would have been the tyrant sorcerer," he said in a gruff voice.

"Yes. Probably he would have lied to me, said our kingdom was under attack and he needed me to cast my spells to destroy the enemy. But what difference would my ignorance make to those I would have killed or harmed? No difference, so a tyrant I would have been." She drew another long, shuddering breath. "When I understood what he'd done, I attacked him—though not with magic. My mother taught me never to use spells that weren't contained by wards, so no innocents were harmed in the scaling. Instead I went after him with a dagger, but I was no warrior. And he plunged it into my heart instead."

Aruk went rigid. "*What?*"

"My mother saved me." Tears wavered through her voice. "Her magic was bound with the rune, so she used blood magic to heal me. That was when I learned what it was, because never did she teach it to me. That scaling, she survived. A small cut only opened over her own breast. Then in her rage, she used blood magic against my father—the scaling killed her. But the spell didn't even touch him. We didn't know that he wore wards to protect himself. Perhaps fearing that one day I might turn on him with my magic. But I never turned on him again."

"Not where he could see," Aruk said.

"No." Pain clogged her throat. "He branded me with the mark because although I would not use my magic to further his ambitions, my usefulness wasn't over. I could be bred to produce another child with magic—and if I was bred to someone who also had magic, even more powerful the child would be. But Solegius of Aremond's power had been rising, and that sorcerer had most of the strong magic users in these southern realms killed so no one might stand against him. And my father did not want to settle for a someone such as a mere healer."

"That is why you told me to cover my ward and never to return." Realization pushed through the harsh mask his expression had become. "Because I am from the Dead Lands, and any child of mine would hold strong magic."

"Yes," she whispered. "He would have captured you, tied you to a bed, and bred you to me—and perhaps bred you to many other women, too. Just in case my child turned out as disappointing to him as I did."

"You are *no* disappointment," Aruk said forcefully, holding her face in his hands. "So you stayed to save those who he tried to execute. When did you decide to run?"

"When he found Prince Wanieer. No powerful magic does that prince have, but my father is desperate. So I became desperate, too." So desperate, she'd spelled the ship and spent two months drowning in her lungs. "My father's wards meant that my magic couldn't touch him, and I couldn't fight him with a sword, so I went in search of someone who could help."

And it was Aruk she'd found. A man whom she'd fallen in love with. A man who might no longer want to take this job, now that he knew she'd used blood magic over and over again.

Her heart aching, she hesitantly asked, "Will you still help me?"

"I will," he vowed hoarsely. "I will kill him for you."

Tremulously she smiled, and closed her eyes in sheer relief, before pressing a grateful kiss to his lips. "Thank you, Aruk. I would have done *anything*. But I'm so glad it will be you."

He nodded, his jaw clenching. "But no more blood magic. Whatever needs done, we will find another way. Not one that risks your life every time."

Jalisa could not make that promise. "Some things are worth risking my life for."

"And you have hired me to risk mine. So no more blood magic. We will end your father without it."

She nodded. "If we can."

"We *can*," he said fiercely, then paused and gave her

a wry look. "As soon as we get off this island."

Jalisa laughed. "Yes," she agreed. "I think we must do that first."

ARUK the FETTERED

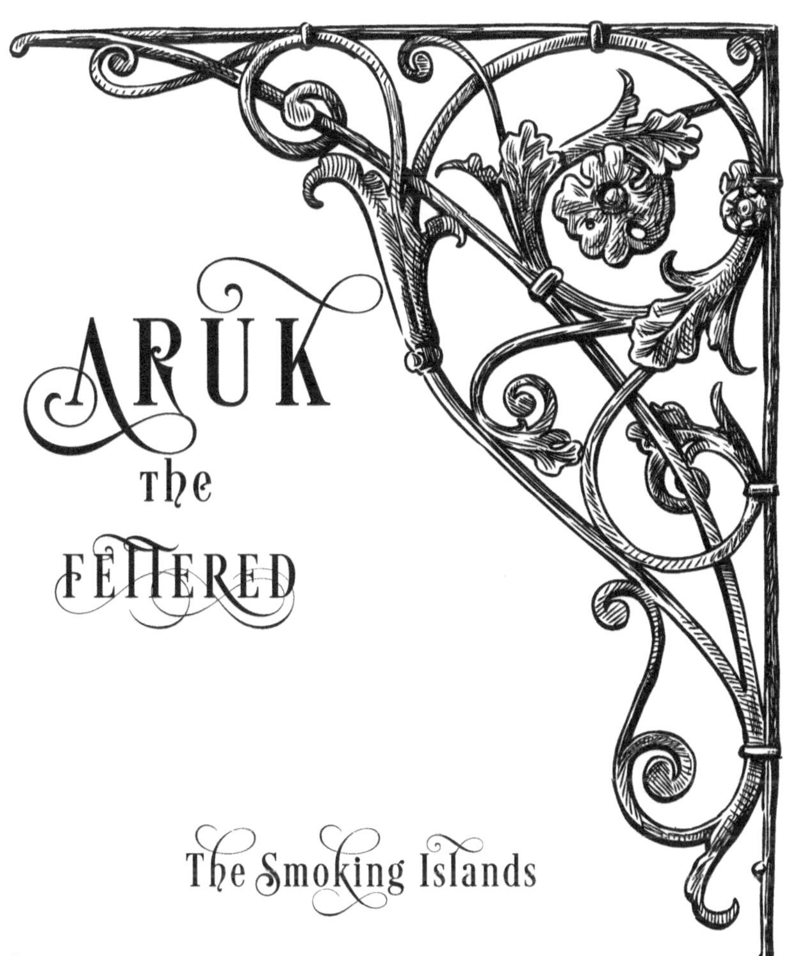

The Smoking Islands

ARUK WOULD HAVE GIVEN ANYTHING TO STAY FOREVER on this island with his princess. Jalisa was nothing like the fantasy woman he'd conjured as a companion the first six months he'd been stranded here. Instead she was far more incredible than he'd ever imagined. Never had she complained of the roughness of their living or the work they must do. Always she helped when she could—and when she could not, some other task she would complete for him. She made him laugh and made him think and made him smile and made him ache with need for her.

But never would she be happy here. Not while her

kingdom lived under her father's heel. Worry for her people would consume her, and never would she abandon them.

Just as Aruk would never abandon his duty. So similar they were, though it had taken him so very long to see.

Not much longer would he have to see her at all. He'd recovered canvas and timbers from the wreckage of her ship, then remade the dinghy to sail and added projecting floats to stabilize it. Another day or two would cure the resin that waterproofed the outrigger hulls, and then they would set out for Savadon.

Where she believed that Aruk would kill her father in exchange for one night with her. Yet that was not what Aruk would do.

Kill her father, yes. But Jalisa had already paid enough. No more blood would Aruk ask her to shed in her search for freedom.

The sun was high when he returned from a short hunt to the hut—which was empty. To the beach Aruk went in search of his princess, slowing as he saw Jalisa shedding her silk shift and walking into the turquoise water.

This cove was well-sheltered by a reef, the waves gentle and waters calm. Yet she had not often bathed in the water—not when the salt stung her wound. Now her sleek golden skin was bared to the sun, only slightly paler over her back and ass. Her hair was not so wild as it had been when she'd first arrived on the island. Aruk had carved a comb for her, and every night she untangled the snarls. Still the dark tresses hung in thick, messy waves to the upper swell of her ass.

He recalled the woman at the parade who had risked a trampling simply to see Jalisa's beauty, and thinking that beauty was not worth as much as gold. Yet now Aruk would have crossed oceans to look upon his princess.

So beautiful she was. Yet Jalisa's true beauty was not her face; instead it was her warm and generous heart.

A heart so generous, it might have killed her.

In all of his travels, Aruk had seen many warriors—men and women—fight and bleed to protect their homes. He'd seen them sacrifice their lives to defend the people they loved. He'd risked his own life many times, and not always for love. Sometimes simply for gold or for adventure.

Yet the risk Jalisa had taken…in Aruk's experience, almost always it seemed to be women who sacrificed themselves in that quiet way. Almost always it was mothers and wives. Most did not use magic, but it was the same. Silently bleeding as they did what needed to be done. Always giving pieces of themselves to others, without keeping anything for their own.

Mothers and wives…and now a woman who would be queen. And Aruk had thought her selfish when she'd spoken of having something for her own. She had simply wanted a life where she was not always bleeding for everyone else. Still she would be kind and generous—but she wanted something for herself, too.

True freedom, she'd called it. Aruk would do anything to see her have that freedom. For she was worth so very much. He was nowhere near worthy of her.

Yet he could not stay away.

He shed the rag around his hips at the water's edge. She had seen him bathe too many times in this cove to be surprised by his nudity, so when she turned to him, it was with a warm and welcoming smile.

"Join me! The water is so fine!"

As was Jalisa. Waist-deep she stood, two long locks of wet hair hanging forward over her shoulders and veiling her breasts, the waves lapping gently at her stomach. Waist-deep for Jalisa barely covered the hot rise of Aruk's cock. Farther out he waded before facing her.

Her gaze slipped downward before lifting again, soft color in her cheeks as she laughed at him. "You returned from your hunt too quickly! I have been caught being lazy."

She was never lazy. If she had been, they would not already have a store of fruit and smoked fish ready for their voyage. "We only need enough meat for this night and tomorrow. So it did not take long."

"Oh." The laughter in her eyes dimmed and she sighed. "Yes."

"Do you wish to stay longer?" Aruk would. But he did not truly think she wanted to.

She confirmed that with a small shake of her head. Softly she said, "It is just…so lovely this island has been."

"Yes," he agreed gruffly, chest aching.

Eyes downcast, she skimmed her fingers through the water in idle swirls. "You must be eager to rejoin the tournament finally."

"I am not. But I must rejoin my brother and carry out our duty."

"You are not rejoining the tournament?" She looked up, brows arched imperiously. "Then what is the duty that will take you away from me, warrior?"

That would *take* him away from her. As if he belonged to her.

As he did. "To make certain no one brings Khides' gauntlet back to Solegius."

Her lips parted. "Khides' gauntlet is the relic they seek? My mother told me the legend of that weapon and of the brothers who broke the world. If it fell into the hands of a tyrant such as Solegius…"

Jalisa trailed off, as if every word she would choose to describe the horror of that was simply not horrific enough.

"Strax and I are bound by a blood obligation to see that no one unworthy ever wields it," he told her. "And the gauntlet's location is well-guarded…but I have to be certain none of the contestants wins the gauntlet and brings the weapon back to that sorcerer."

"And so you *must* go," she whispered thickly.

Throat constricted, Aruk nodded.

Through her lashes, her downcast gaze shimmered as brightly as the waters when she hesitantly said, "When you are certain the gauntlet is safe, warrior…would you return to Savadon?"

Hoarsely he admitted, "I know of nothing that might

keep me away. Though more than a year might pass before I can return. The keep where the gauntlet is held lies six months' journey away."

A shuddering breath left her. As if in pain and relief, her eyes closed and the tears slipped over her cheeks. "I do not care how long it will be."

Aruk did. Because every moment apart would be agony.

But *these* moments they had.

He surged through the water and eagerly she met him, lifting her mouth for his kiss. Catching her, Aruk hauled her up against his chest, her face level with his and her legs circling his waist. Salt from the sea and her tears flavored his first taste of her, then only her sweetness and heat as he licked his way past her lips. Her fingers tangled in his hair and fiercely she returned his kiss, his princess taking something for herself.

Aruk would give to her all that he had. Hungrily he consumed her mouth, slanting his lips over hers again and again until the low moan in her throat was a constant refrain. Greedily she met his kiss, lick for lick, then broke away, her gaze searching his as her heaving breaths swept over his lips.

Shakily she whispered, "I want more than one night, Aruk. I want *every* night until you have to leave."

Nights not spent as payment or fee but in shared need. No sacrifice would it require. Only when it was over would they bleed.

"You will have every night," he vowed harshly and

began carrying her toward the shore. "And the days, too. Every moment that remains, I will have you so hard and so long, you will still feel me within you when I am gone."

The word *gone* seemed to pierce her through. A gasping sob escaped her and she kissed him again, deep and hard, hands fisted in his hair. Branding herself on him. Sinking so deep under his skin. So that he would always feel her, too.

Aruk wouldn't feel anything *but* her. Nothing but the way she filled his heart so full.

Beyond the waves, his feet sank into warm sand. Urgently she moved against him, stiffening his erection to throbbing steel. So hard he meant to fuck her. But no pleasure would she know with those rough grains abrading her every soft and wet crevice. Yet if he didn't ease his need before taking her to the hut, their first time would be over the minute he sank his cock into her scorching embrace.

So hot she was. And so blessed he was, to ever know her thus.

Lowering her onto the silk shift she'd discarded on the sand, Aruk followed her down, and a tortured groan ripped from him when she eagerly spread her thighs to make room for his hips. His body shook with the need to accept that blatant invitation. Molten seed overfilled his sac, burning up the length of his shaft and dripping from the crown.

But only a small taste would he take now. Only a

small taste.

Her cunt glistened with her arousal, tight and pink and lush. Braced above her, Aruk fisted his aching length. Through her sultry folds, he slicked the head of his cock up and down, teasing her entrance before pressing forward through her cunt lips and over the top of her cleft, his long thick shaft riding over her clit. Beneath him, Jalisa cried out in frustration, her hips angling upward as if to draw him down to her entrance again.

So that he might sink his cock into her, again and again.

Not yet. His mouth claimed the wonder of hers as he stroked again over the slick heat of her cunt. Faster, over her clit with each thrust. Soon she no longer tried to lure him inside but moved with him, legs tight around his waist and her body arching beneath his. Sobbing gasps of pleasure she breathed into their kiss, then all at once she threw her head back and cried his name, her slim torso a quivering bow with plucked string.

Grunting, Aruk followed her into that release, seed spurting over her belly. Then chest heaving, he kissed her. Soon he would rise with Jalisa in his arms and carry her into the sea to rinse the abrasive sand from her skin before continuing to the hut. Not much time did they have to waste.

But time spent kissing her was never time wasted.

Her lips were swollen and smiling when he lifted his head. Then she frowned and her brow pleated…as she heard what he suddenly did.

The rhythmic splash of oars. The creaking of boats. A petulant voice drifting over the water.

"…do you think I will still have her now? After we have all watched that barbarian defile her? Better that I had never cast the spell that let you find this cursed island!"

Jalisa scrambled out from beneath him, eyes panicked. Blindly she fumbled for her shift, shaking loose sand from the silk. Aruk turned to look as she dragged it over her head.

Twelve boats full of armed soldiers—and the vessel at their head also carried three men in silks. One with a protruding bottom lip as petulant as the words he'd spoken. One with a weasel's sly air and his hot eyes fixed on Jalisa. The other with rigid face whose narrowed eyes returned Aruk's gaze before he looked down at Aruk's side, where his ward softly glowed.

"Your father?" Aruk guessed.

"With his pig advisor Fin Ketles and the prince." Frantically Jalisa tugged on his arm. "We must run."

"Where to?"

"The hut." With desperate strength, she tried again to drag him up. "There I will cast a spell that—"

With her blood? Urgently Aruk caught her arms. "*Never* like this, Jalisa. *Never* in fear and to harm. The scaling is always unknown but that is more certain to scale larger. You must have seen. Your mother saved you out of love and the scaling was small, but she died when she attacked your father. And your worst scaling was when you spelled the ship in fear and desperation to leave. Swear to me you never will."

"But—"

"Swear to me!"

"I swear it!" she shouted at him, then her terrified gaze swung past Aruk to the water. "Then what do we do? We cannot fight this many."

In time, Aruk could. He only needed to flee with her to the jungle that grew on the mountain—and as the soldiers pursued them, he would hunt them and kill them one by one. Or ten by ten. It mattered not to him.

Yet such a plan put Jalisa at high risk. In the confusion of the jungle, a soldier might mistake her for Aruk when loosing an arrow. As they ran and hid, more likely would she be injured. And when he left her to hunt the soldiers, she would be unprotected—not just from her father, but from the fanged predators that stalked the mountainside.

"We will surrender to him," Aruk said.

Jalisa looked at him as if he'd gone mad. "*Surrender* to him?"

"You did not defy him. I laid eyes upon your beauty and stole you from Savadon. Here on this island, I held you prisoner and mercilessly ravaged you against your will."

Eyes filled with tears, she shook her head. "Aruk, no. He will—"

"Kill me?" No. It was her father who would die. As Aruk had vowed to her. "He will keep me alive."

Her swimming gaze fell to the glowing rune at his

side. Helplessly she shook her head. "Let me instead—"

"*No,*" he snarled. "You risk sacrificing everything. What I propose sacrifices nothing. He will not harm you. And he will do no real harm to me."

Agony filled her face as she implored him, "Please, Aruk. He will chain you like an animal."

"Chain me, he might. Imprison me and keep me away from you?" Aruk smiled with grim determination. "He can try. Now rip away from my grasp and race toward the water, screaming for rescue. Then do not watch any of what occurs after."

"No, Aruk, *please*," she sobbed, beating at his chest. "Please. I love you."

His heart swelled so fiercely his entire soul ached with it. Such a sweet ache.

"Then I have strength to survive anything. As you will, princess, for so much do I love you in return," he told her gruffly, and her wondering gaze lifted to his. Her sobbing breaths eased, and he saw the hope and determination in her that matched his own. "Now, go."

After one last lingering look at his face, Jalisa yanked free of his hold and fled. From the king's boat came the shouted order to take the barbarian alive.

Naked, Aruk turned to face the soldiers surging up onto the beach. Lifting his arms wide, he grinned at them. "Come on, then!"

Because surrender, he would. But not until he unleashed upon them his fury and pain at sending Jalisa back to her father, even for a moment. So he did not surrender until the golden beach was soaked in blood.

Better their blood—and his—than Jalisa's.

On the red sands Aruk finally kneeled, and let the soldiers put chains upon him, then let them beat him to the ground with clubs and boots. Into the dark hold of the king's ship he was tossed, in fetters, imprisoned.

But Jalisa loved him. So not once in the long, painful days that followed did Aruk's grin fade from his bloodied lips.

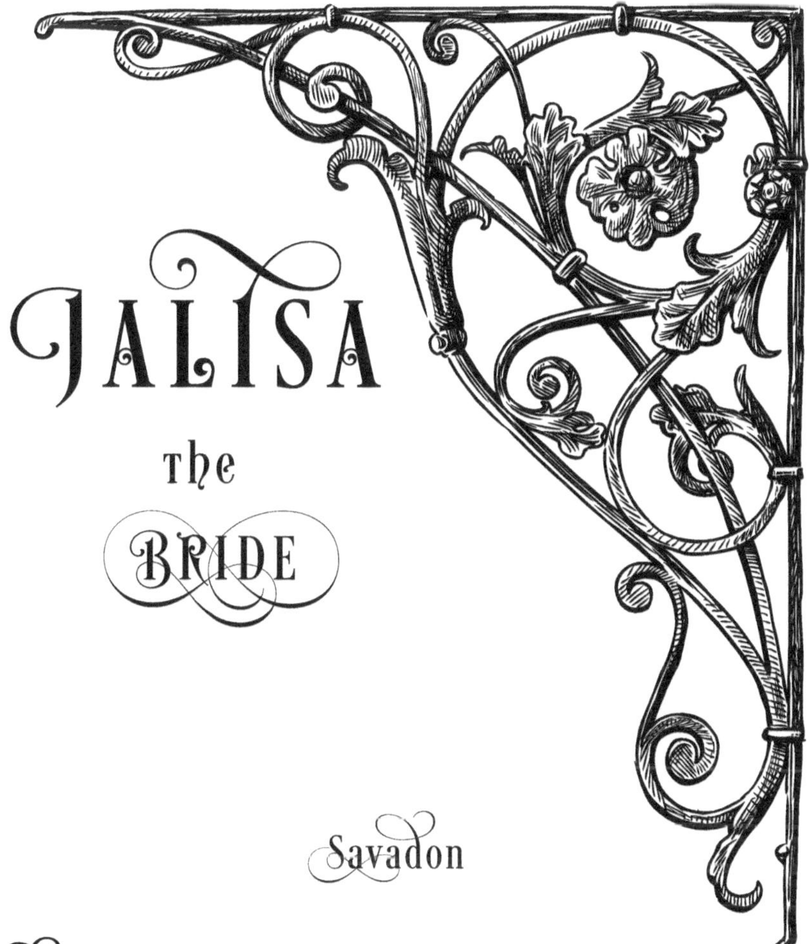

Jalisa the Bride

Savadon

Such a pretty bride she was.

With dull eyes, Jalisa stared at herself in the polished silver mirror as the maid secured her tiara atop sleek, shining tresses. Her golden tan had not faded, but was hidden beneath a pale powder. Aruk's kisses no longer swelled her lips. As if the island had never been.

But it *had* been. And Aruk loved her. So she would not despair.

Even though tonight, she would marry another.

No notice had she been given of the wedding except for her maids scurrying in to make her ready. So it seemed that, in spite of watching her be ravished by a barbarian, Prince Wanieer must have agreed to marry her. Because she was not what Wanieer wanted, anyway. Her kingdom was.

And her father only cared that she was bred. No doubt he believed that Aruk had already taken care of that part. So proud he'd seemed of her for catching Aruk's eye and—for all that her father knew—for being abducted and raped. As if Jalisa had deliberately set herself up as bait to catch her father a warrior from the Dead Lands and to be impregnated with his powerful seed.

But the child needed to be legitimate, so Jalisa must be wed. And in Savadon, after every royal wedding came the royal bedding—a ceremony witnessed by officials who confirmed consummation had been completed.

Consummation with the odious Wanieer.

Jalisa closed her eyes. She would *not* cast spells in rage and fear. She would not.

But she might vomit on him. Not such a pretty bride would she be then.

And if not vomit, something else. Jalisa *would* think of a way to stop this wedding—and attempt an escape that would take her down to the dungeon and free Aruk.

The sacrifice he'd made would not be in vain. Because although he'd told her not to look back at what happened on the beach…she had looked. She had seen. A great fighter he was. Yet still he'd been brought to his knees. Beaten.

Her heart had been screaming ever since. Screaming

for her to fight, to run. All that kept her compliant was the terror of what her father might do to Aruk if she rebelled against him.

The time came to be escorted to the ceremonial chambers—and never had she wished for her father's company, but now she did because her escort was Fin Ketles. His attentions toward her had never been subtle. Yet ever since he'd witnessed her on the beach with Aruk, it was as if he believed seeing her naked meant that she belonged to him now in some way. As if the brief ecstasy she'd found with the man she loved had been only a show put on to tease Fin Ketles.

That possessive gaze swept her the moment they stepped into the corridor. His eyes settled on her breasts. "How beautiful you are, princess."

She ignored him and continued on, needing no escort to find the chambers. Never had the ceremonial chambers been used in her lifetime, but it was one of her favorite rooms within the palace. There was the altar room where a ribbon would be tied around her hand, binding her to Wanieer. There was the large, open bedchamber with discreet nooks for the observers to sit in. None of those did she ever spend time in. Instead she always opened the doors to the enormous balcony. The palace had been built on a cliff overlooking Savadon's busy bay, and on that balcony she could see so far north over the Illwind Sea, and so far south through the rolling hills. Her view west was obstructed by mountains, yet they were also so beautiful—and when the sun set, the snowy peaks were painted in such incredible hues of rose and gold.

Fin Ketles' voice demanded her attention again. "I will be one of the observers tonight," he said gleefully. "So this will be the second time I see you fucked."

Jaw set, Jalisa heard nothing. *He* was nothing.

"Or perhaps I won't," the advisor smirked. "I do not know that your groom will be able to complete this consummation. No woman—or man—has yet been able to get a rise from him. So perhaps your father will have me take his place."

No rise from Prince Wanieer? Perhaps that was yet another reason why her father had been so unbothered by what Aruk claimed to have done to her. The prince couldn't have bred her, anyway.

And despite the advisor's hope, she had no fear that her father would let Fin Ketles touch her. For the king had but one purpose: to get strong sorcerers from her. As horrible as that purpose was, at least it protected her from his advisor, who had no magic at all.

Head high, she entered the ceremonial chambers. Her step faltered. A dozen soldiers from the palace guard stood near the bedchamber. There was no sign of Prince Wanieer. Only the magistrate in his dark robes, and her father—who was in consultation with the master of the guard.

The trail end of the guard's assurance she heard. "… these new chains are twice as thick. He will not break them so easily."

Aruk. Chained with arms and legs outspread, naked on the enormous bed. His bruised left eye was half closed, his jaw swollen and lips split.

Yet as her eyes met his, he grinned.

"So my daughter is here," her father said abruptly. "Now we must find a way to get a rise out of him."

"Slyworm powder?" Fin Ketles suggested.

Her father nodded, turning to look at Aruk. "We'll force it down his throat if we must…" He paused, for Aruk's cock no longer lay heavily against his thigh. "Or perhaps my daughter's beauty is all that was needed. Go to him then, Jalisa, and put your hand to his. We will not use the altar this night."

To marry them. To marry Jalisa…to Aruk.

Just as her father had married her mother, simply to legitimize the heir. And then he'd enslaved his unacknowledged queen with chains made from her love for Jalisa.

So, too, could Jalisa see the same happening to Aruk. His love for her would bind him stronger than any iron chain. That he would be trapped, as she had been, in the role that her father had decided for him. With no freedom, and no choice. And soon drugged so that other women could be bred on him.

None of it would Jalisa ever allow.

Heart thundering, she approached the bed. His gaze devoured her, as if he'd been as starved for the sight of her as she had been for him. His arms were outspread, chained to the corner posts. Thick iron cuffs circled his wrists, the skin beneath raw. Pain lodged in her throat as she climbed onto the bed, kneeling beside him, and placed her hand against his.

And how was she supposed to act now? As if he were a barbarian who'd forced her?

She supposed it didn't really matter anymore. Yet she spoke quietly enough that her voice would not carry to her father and his advisor, observing from near the bedchamber's entrance.

"You are bare again, warrior," she said softly.

His grin didn't spread as she expected it to. Instead his smile faded and his voice was hoarse as he told her, "You don't want to be a bride. I will refuse the vow."

And be beaten again? No.

"I said that I would like to choose," she reminded him. "And to marry a man that I love. So I will happily be your bride, Aruk."

His eyes blazed. "Then where is that magistrate?"

Approaching warily with crimson ribbon in hand, Jalisa took a moment to look at the chains that held Aruk to the bed. Truly thick they were.

"Did you break your chains in attempt to escape?"

"And come for you. I was near to it before the guards rushed me. And like a fool, in that small cell I swung the broken chain at them instead of lashing it like a whip." A dull flush climbed his cheeks, as if in embarrassment and shame. "It matters not. A full night we will be bound together in this bed. I will break them again—or the bones in my hands. One way or another, Jalisa, this night you will be free."

A full night—because the ribbon that the magistrate weaved through their fingers now could not be untied until dawn, or their marriage would also be undone.

The magistrate looked across the chamber to her father, who called out, "Begin!"

To Jalisa, the magistrate spoke her string of royal names before asking, "Do you pledge yourself to this man and swear to be his faithful wife?"

So very fast and dizzying her pulse was, rushing the blood through her veins. "I will."

"And you, barbarian—"

"Aruk of the Dead Lands, son of the Fang Clan, Keeper of the Sacred Oath," Aruk said in a raw voice. "And 'warrior' to this woman who will be my wife."

"Do you pledge yourself to this woman and swear to be her faithful husband?"

Fiercely he vowed, "*Always* I will."

"Then upon a kiss that seals your vows, you shall be wife and husband."

So swiftly Jalisa claimed him, bending over to capture his mouth beneath hers. So sweetly he kissed her in return, silently echoing the vow he'd just spoken, his love heating and sweetening every tender caress of his lips.

"Now shed the wedding gown, daughter, and mount him."

Jalisa froze. Dread and sickness coiled beneath her heart—where moments before, only joy and love had resided.

"Wife." Aruk's low, rough voice brought her gaze to his. "There is only me."

Only Aruk. Her husband. With trembling fingers she unlaced the ties at the top of her shoulders. Bound hands meant that everyday gowns could not be so easily removed—and the observers could not have fabric concealing the consummation. So her wedding gown had been designed for simple removal, and included a gossamer undergown that allowed her to stay covered while not truly hiding anything beneath.

Aruk groaned as she revealed her breasts, her taut nipples beaded beneath the glimmering fabric. "No taste have I had yet, wife."

Right arm outstretched to his, she braced her left beside his head and bent over him. Hungrily he latched on to her nipple through the gossamer, sucking at that taut peak.

Pleasure shuddered through her. So hot his mouth was. Every flick of his tongue and pull upon her breast filled her entire body with liquid fire.

"With their hands bound," her father said, "more slack is needed in that chain. She is not tall enough to stretch over him."

Pleasure fled.

"Only me, wife," Aruk rumbled softly against her breast.

"Only me. Now bring your sweet cunt to my mouth, or never will your virgin sheath stretch easily for my cock."

Only with more slack in the chain could this be done. But those guards were not here, Jalisa told herself. Only Aruk. With heat and tongue, she kissed her husband as one guard placed the point of his sword against Aruk's throat and two others carefully unfastened the chain from the bed post. They doled out more length before swiftly locking it again.

"Now mount him, daughter." Impatience hardened her father's voice.

"I am not ready!" she snapped back over her shoulder. "Look at the size of him! He will tear me apart."

"I will find oil to rub on her cunt," Fin Ketles suggested.

"Rub it instead on your cock and then set it afire," Jalisa hissed. "You will *never* touch me, you rotting codpiece."

"To my mouth, wife," Aruk growled. "Now."

She did, lifting the gossamer hem so she might see his face. His gaze locked upon hers as his mouth locked over her cunt. His tongue slicked and teased and there was pleasure here again, swimming through her in hot waves. But there was rage, too. Rage that he was chained. Rage that she was forced to do this.

Softly he kissed her clit. "Only me, wife."

Only him. Only the love she had for him, pressing away all the rage and fear. She let that sweet emotion fill her, until there was nothing but Aruk and how much she loved him. Wet lust slicked her inner thighs as she moved down to straddle his stomach, yet it was only love that Jalisa tasted when she kissed his mouth, glistening with her arousal.

Only love on her lips as she said to him again those words. "I love you, Aruk." And that love was on her lips when Jalisa rose over his cock and spoke different words, but they still had the same meaning. That she loved him.

And she would free him.

His big body tensed as she fitted the broad head of his cock to her virgin entrance. Realization flared over his battered face. "No, Jalisa—!"

With his name on her lips, she took the full length of his shaft into her cunt with one hard downward stroke. Pain speared through her, a hot flare at her entrance as her maidenhead tore and spilled her virgin's blood, a burning pressure where his thickness wedged deep inside her.

So deep inside her.

With a ragged cry, she fell forward, bracing her hands on his chest. His heart thundered under her palms.

"Jalisa!" Hoarsely he called her name. "My wife, my princess. Tell me you are well."

Chest heaving, she looked up at him. "So very well."

His gaze searched hers, then down the length of her body, and she read the question he did not ask.

"I cannot tell what the scaling was," she whispered huskily. All she could feel was his cock inside her sheath. Her head rolled back and unable to help herself, she swiveled her hips, stirring his heavy shaft deep within.

"Oh, my husband. You feel so good."

"Then use me for your pleasure, wife," he said in a low and urgent voice. "And tell to me the spell."

"To weaken a link in each chain," she gasped, rising and falling. "You're so deep inside me, Aruk."

"And there I will stay, for this crimson ribbon I will not unbind. But you must hold tight."

So she would. Rising the length of his cock, she kissed him before sliding back down, her inner muscles clinging to the thick shaft spearing the full depth of her cunt.

Aruk groaned beneath her, and it was but the rumble of a deeper roar that built within him, vibrating through his chest. With a mighty heave, he snapped the chains holding his arms and legs.

Then her father got a true rise from him, as Aruk arose from the bed with death in his eyes. Jalisa clung to him with her left arm circling his neck, her legs wrapped around his hips, and his cock buried deep. With their hands bound together, she knew he would not be wielding a weapon with it. Instead he locked his forearm over the small of her back, and though that made Jalisa hold her own arm at an awkward angle, it was not a painful one.

"Watch none of what happens next," he commanded harshly, as brusque orders from her father joined the frantic shouts of the guards.

Jalisa buried her face in his shoulder and closed her eyes. The powerful surge of his body shoved his cock deeper. She moaned against his neck, then gasped when a sudden pivot swung her around with him and her clit rubbed against him where they were pressed so tightly together. Screams she heard, yet none of it louder than the pounding of her blood, her heaving breaths. Only once she looked up, to see a soldier's face wiped from the front of his skull by the whip of the heavy chain as Aruk fought for their future, their freedom.

A sharp lunge was a deep, hard stroke inside her. Jalisa began to shake, frantically tasting his skin, showering his neck with hot openmouthed kisses. Suddenly all became still and quiet, except for a nearby wheezing.

"Where did the weasel go?" Aruk demanded. "The one who thought he might rub my wife's cunt."

"Don't…know…"

That wheezing answer was her father's. Jalisa lifted her head to see that Aruk had the bloodied chain wrapped around his throat.

To her, Aruk said, "Are you certain?"

She buried her face against his neck again. "Yes," she whispered.

"Then come for me, wife." His forearm tightened, holding her in place for a strong upward thrust. "Come for me as I fulfill this vow I made to you."

Sinking into her, again and again. The drenched slide of his cock driving her higher and higher, tighter and tighter. Barely did she hear the thud of a body to the floor, then Aruk's hand was buried in her hair and he was kissing her, fucking her, and it was more sweet pleasure than she could bear. She came hard, her sheath clasping him so tight, his name a scream from her lips. Then he slowed, and held her close, breath mingling.

With his seed not within her, but splashed hotly over her belly. Because Aruk would not spend inside her unless he could stay.

Heart aching, she searched his dark eyes. "You have wife and kingdom now, Aruk." Two things her warrior had said that he could not have. "But will it only be for one night?"

No answer he gave, except to kiss her and to carry her to bed.

ARUK the UNBOUND

Savadon

As dawn crept across the sky, Aruk knew that he would not leave his wife.

But he had known it before—on bloodied sands and in chains. Perhaps he had known longer than that, from the long days when she'd still been recovering from the wound in her side, and she'd told him of Savadon's war-torn history.

Now his fingers lightly skimmed over the scar that wound had left as Jalisa lay sleepily atop his chest. Their hands were still bound, but although dawn had come, he was in no hurry to unwind their marriage ribbon.

After the second time he'd had her, she'd called for the bodies and his chains to be taken away. In the ceremonial chamber they'd remained, with its balcony that seemed to open up to the sky…and look down into the bay that was the heart of Savadon.

"Might I set up a watch up along the docks?" he asked softly.

"You are king," she murmured against his throat. "You can do anything you like. Who would you be looking for?"

"Tournament contestants returning to Aremond." For they would have to pass through Savadon to reach that kingdom. As all trade to the realms south of the Illwind Sea did. "Little sense it makes now to go chasing after them. Our paths might too easily cross—especially if they sail south as I sail north. But I know the names and faces of all the warriors who entered the tournament. Their descriptions I could give to the watch. So if my brother has failed…then it would be I who makes certain the gauntlet never reaches Solegius's hands."

"And so you would still fulfill your duty." Her voice sounded thick. "But also you would stay?"

"Yes." Though he must tell her, "If I ever hear again that the gauntlet might fall into unworthy hands, I would have to go. Though it does not happen often. This is the first time in six generations that warriors of the Fang Clan were called to our sacred duty."

"If you go, then I would, too. We would leave Savadon in a good advisor's hands, and an adventure I would have.

And so you are staying?"

Her voice broke. And that was the second time she had asked—as if she had not believed the first. Rolling her onto her back, he saw the tears on her lashes.

"Did you think I might not? You are my heart, Jalisa."

"I knew not if you would have a choice. And you did not spend inside me."

He brushed away her tears. "Because you said not to."

She blinked. "I did?"

"You asked me not to when you hired me. And said you wanted to choose when you would have children, to wait until you were ready." Which Aruk had no argument with. This was the freedom his wife needed. So he would give it to her.

"Oh." She softly bit her full bottom lip. "With you, all is different. I am ready now."

Never had his cock hardened so fast. And she laughed at him as he spread her legs and pushed inside her, but on the next thrust her laugh turned to a pleasured gasp. Then she joined him, racing to the end with her cunt clutching his pumping shaft, coming helplessly beneath him as he endlessly filled her with his hot seed.

For a longer time he kissed her, but the day could not be delayed much longer. Savadon was waking up to a new queen—and king—and so much would need to be done.

Aruk untied the ribbon, then tied it again around his wrist. To the balcony he walked to relieve himself over the railing, while Jalisa groaned and moaned her way to the privy cupboard. A clever design that was, with a waste shaft that emptied over the cliff—though she had told him that when the wind blew strong enough, it might blow the piss right back up the shaft and onto the person seated there.

So when she gave a short scream, he briefly wondered if that was what had happened. Yet there was not even a breeze. Frowning, he turned as she burst out of the privy—where the weasel advisor was climbing out of the shaft, knife in hand. All night he must have hidden in that waste shaft, because Aruk had himself looked into the privy cupboard in search of him.

Blood thundering, he surged toward her—but not before the weasel caught her by the hair and jerked her back against him, knife at her throat.

"She was mine!" the weasel wailed. "And if I cannot have her, no one will!"

Aruk fell to his knees, meeting Jalisa's panicked gaze. "Anything you wish," he begged hoarsely. "Anything—"

Heart rending in two, Aruk watched the blade slash across her throat. A primal scream ripped from his chest and in the next moment he was on his feet and—

Jalisa still stood, unbleeding. Looking as stunned as he.

The weasel slashed again and the sound was like steel scraping over iron.

"The scaling," Aruk told her, beginning to grin. "You weakened the iron chain by stealing weakness from yourself—and gained iron's strength."

"Scaling?" the weasel exclaimed. "What scal—"

That was as far as he got before Jalisa whipped around and punched him in the throat. Gasping, he fell back. With a scream of rage, she struck with her knee between his legs, sending him reeling out onto the balcony. Then she shoved her dainty foot into his ass and sent him flailing over the railing.

Chest heaving, she looked to Aruk. "I have wanted to do that for *so long.*"

Laughing, he went to her, cupping her cheeks—and feeling in amazement the warm suppleness of her skin. No different it seemed. Yet when she picked up the dagger and drew the blade over her flesh, nowhere could she cut. Not even her tongue, when she tried that.

"No more blood magic," she whispered.

Aruk could not be sorry. No longer would she silently bleed herself to death while giving all that she had to others. Yet he knew that, in Jalisa's eyes, blood magic had been her way of helping—and of not being helpless. "You are queen," he reminded her softly. "With iron skin, so no one might do you harm. You will not need that magic. Other options you will have…and a husband who will always fight for and protect you."

Smiling, she lifted her mouth for a kiss—then drew back to look up at him imperiously. "Many riches we have in this castle, Aruk. Reassure me that I will not find you one day, jerking your cock on a pile of gold coins."

Heartily he laughed and drew her up for that kiss.

"The only promise I will make is that, if I do, they will bear your likeness." Then his heart filled, and he kissed her again. "It was the only likeness I had of you. And when you gave it to me, still warmed it was from your skin. Now I need no gold at all."

For he'd already found the greatest of riches in her.

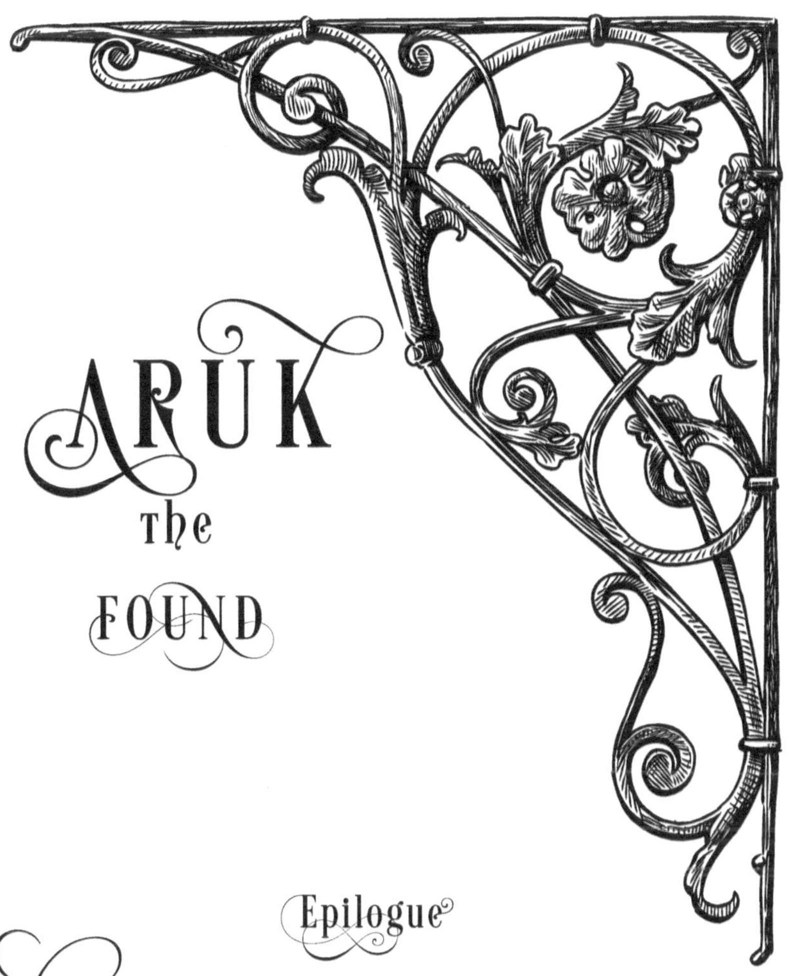

ARUK the FOUND

Epilogue

Here we are again, in the kingdom of Savadon, on the southern coast of the Illwind Sea. Eight months have passed, and on this day, two travelers are escorted from the docks to the palace at the behest of Savadon's king.

Aruk was hardly surprised to see Strax, though lack of surprise was not lack of joy, and fiercely the brothers embraced. More surprising was his companion, Mara, who had hated his brother so fiercely—though after Aruk's own tumultuous path to love, perhaps no surprise it should have been. Full with child Mara was, and the trip across the sea had been difficult for his brother's new wife. Soon it was settled that the pair would stay in Savadon until she gave birth, and was strong enough to continue home.

No arrangement could have pleased Aruk more, to have the people he loved best in the world gathered together. And so proud he introduced his brother to his wife, Queen Jalisa the Ironskin—though some within the palace also called her The Queen Who Rode Her King Into Righteous Battle. No one in Savadon missed her father's rule, and the pretty princess they'd once called spoiled and selfish and difficult had other new names, such as Jalisa the Kind and Jalisa the Generous.

And soon she would also be called a mother.

Of their sacred duty, Strax told him the gauntlet was still safe in Khides' keep. Then Aruk saw the look that passed between Strax and his wife, and knew there must be a story there. Strax laughed and said that a long story it was, a tale of a sorcerer's trap and a midnight wedding, of poisoned lips and skull cliffs and wolf brothers…and you will also hear that that tale, very soon.

Happy months passed in Savadon, with healthy babes born to both couples before Strax and Mara left for her home. But no sad parting it was, for only a few weeks' journey separated their kingdoms, and Jalisa eager to travel and visit.

As the years passed, Aruk and Jalisa took that journey many times with their four children—and other adventures they had, too. Only once did Aruk's duty call him again. Just as she had promised, Jalisa accompanied him—and *great dangers they faced along the way. But that is a tale for anotherwhere and anotherwhen—and this tale has come to an end.*

· END ·

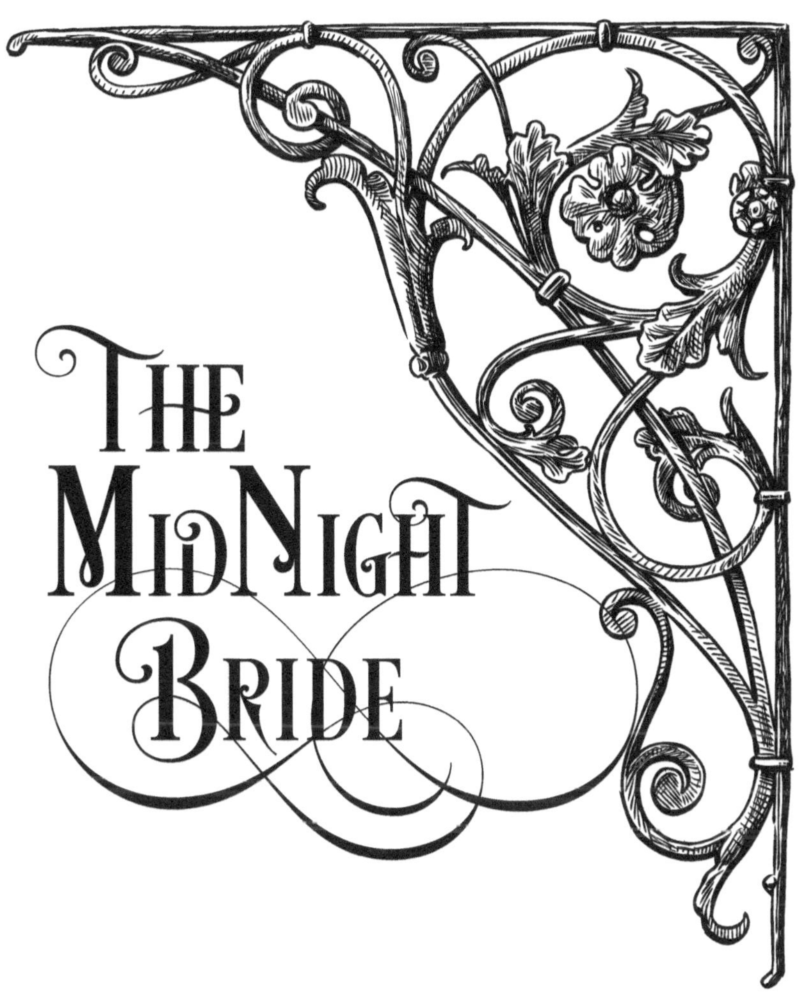

THE MIDNIGHT BRIDE

A DEAD LANDS FANTASY ROMANCE

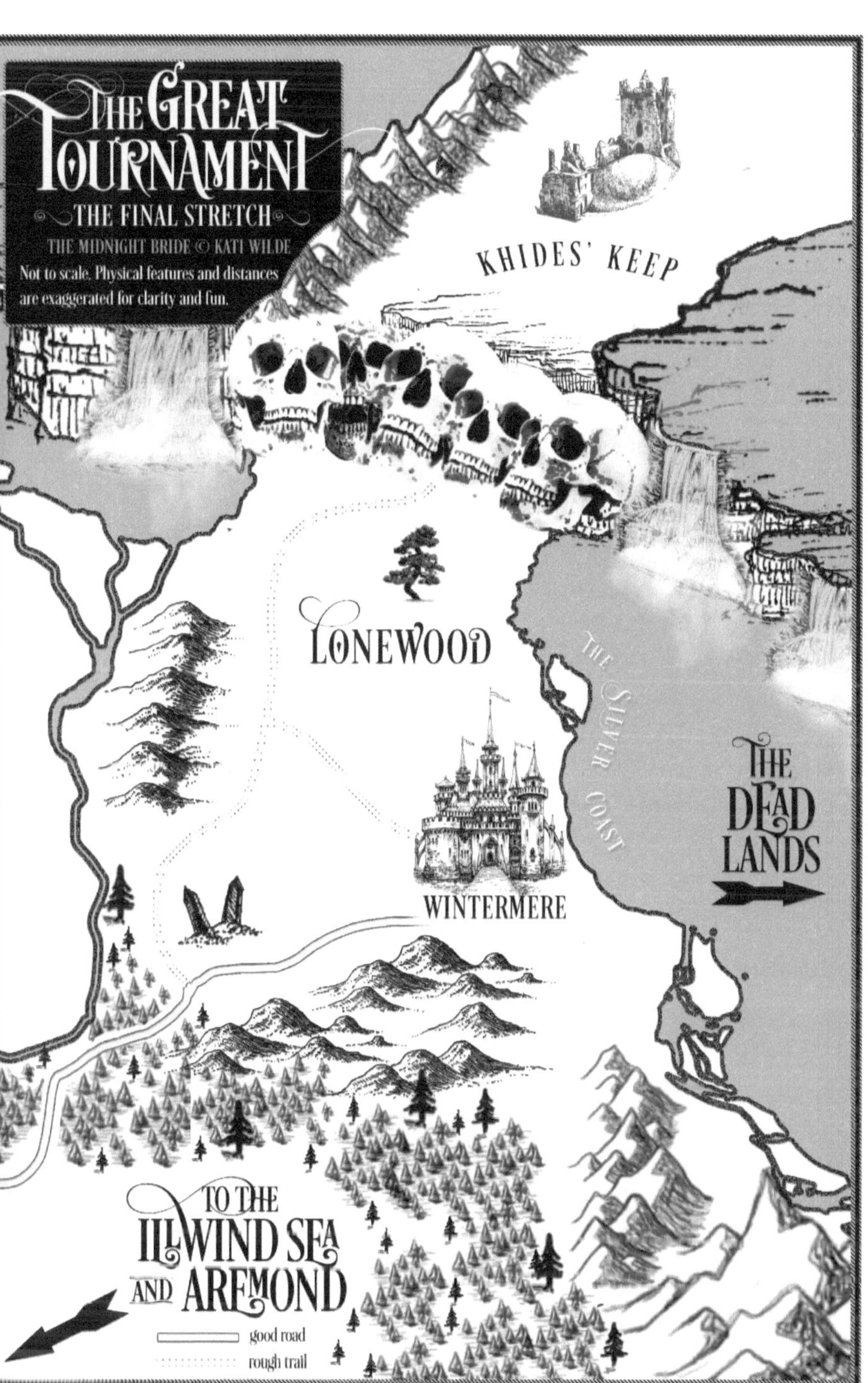

THE GREAT TOURNAMENT
THE FINAL STRETCH
THE MIDNIGHT BRIDE © KATI WILDE
Not to scale. Physical features and distances are exaggerated for clarity and fun.
KHIDES' KEEP
LONEWOOD
THE SILVER COAST
THE DEAD LANDS
WINTERMERE
TO THE ILLWIND SEA AND ARFMOND
good road
rough trail

ERE WE ARE, ONCE AGAIN WEAVING A TALE OF A BRIDE, hoping the words become a spell and make magic. Others have come before—one at midwinter, one stonehearted, one pretty—and still we await the midsummer bride.

But now comes one at midnight.

The time is anotherwhen, a date unknown but nearing the conclusion of a perilous tournament. The place is anotherwhere, a world unnamed but far north of the Illwind Sea. And this story begins, as many stories do, long before our hero and heroine were born. Before ink and parchment, before chisel and stone. So long ago, all that is known of this story's beginning are legends of legends—of two brothers who loved each other, but whose battles broke the world.

Those brothers are not the heroes of this story. Nor are they the villains. Instead they are a warning and a lesson. For we know well the powerful magic that is love.

But sometimes…love is not enough.

STRAX
the
LAST

The Forest Road

THE DAY THAT STRAX'S HEART WAS TORN FROM HIS chest began as every other morning did—he awakened from dreams of Mara with his cock hardened to steel and his hand gripping his sword. Each night, sleep revealed everything he concealed while awake: that his body yearned for Mara's touch as powerfully as his heart yearned to protect her.

But Strax could not help Mara on her quest to retrieve the Gauntlet of Khides. Not without betraying his sacred duty. And with his brother lost to the waves of the Illwind Sea, Strax was the only warrior who could see this journey through to the end.

So when he rose from his furs, Strax didn't cross the short distance between their camps. Instead he broke his fast with a strip of dried venison and watched Mara stir from her own bed. First her head emerged from the furs, and dawn's golden light glinted off the russet strands interwoven through her long dark hair like sparks rising through smoke. Then came her shoulders, clad only in a heavy woven tunic. A quiet moment passed wherein she sat hugging herself against the early morning chill, with her legs still covered and her blankets bunched around her waist.

In the autumn and winter, she'd always leapt out of her furs fully clothed, then quickly saddled her mount. But as spring progressed, she lingered longer and longer in the warmth of her bed.

Strax wished he could interpret Mara's delay as an invitation to join her and truly warm her bed. But the only invitation Strax was likely to receive would be an invitation to stab a sword through his head. She rarely glanced back in his direction—and when she did, no desire burned in her dark eyes. Instead he could only see anger and distrust.

Strax preferred Mara's anger and distrust to what he suspected kept her in that bed, however. In the past weeks, an invisible weight had settled upon her shoulders. Despair, perhaps. Or hopelessness.

It didn't matter what Strax called the burden; only

its cause mattered, and that he could easily guess. Six months past, Mara had entered the king of Aremond's tournament to retrieve Khides' ancient gauntlet from the goddess's stone keep. Three dozen other contestants had joined the race, all hardened warriors—and they had all quickly outpaced her. Within a week, a full day's ride had separated Mara from the pack. Within a month, she traveled faster than she had started out, yet the distance between her and the other contestants had widened.

Yet although she lagged far behind, Mara hadn't given up. Strax had seen the determination that pushed her onto the road each day at first light and kept her there until she fell exhausted into bed each night. He had witnessed her struggle through every obstacle in her path. That she *could* reach Khides' keep, he had no doubt.

But she wouldn't reach it before the others did. To the northeast, the Skull Cliffs were visible in the distance. Not more than a week's ride away, and Khides' keep wasn't much farther than that.

If the gauntlet could be retrieved—and if the guardians at the keep could be defeated—then one of the other contestants probably had it in his possession. Strax would know soon—and so would Mara. There was no other road back to Aremond, so the victor had to ride in this direction to claim his prize. Their paths would soon cross.

So of recent mornings, it seemed that Mara had to force herself to greet a day that might bring her defeat. As if continuing on a quest she'd already lost required more effort from her than simply getting to her feet.

Had Strax not been bound by a blood obligation to stop anyone from winning the tournament, he would have lifted her. He would have carried her.

But he could not.

Instead he called out, "At the speed you move now, woman, a snail will find the gauntlet before you do!"

Her back stiffened. No doubt she was deciding how to respond. Moving quickly meant that his words affected her. But moving slowly proved him right.

As always, she found the response that did neither. Without looking in his direction, she rose smoothly to her feet and called back, "At least I am not the slug in last place, warrior!"

"Today will be the day that I overtake you!" Strax declared heartily. "Then *you* will be last!"

Her dismissive scoff reached his ears, and Strax grinned. Reclining back on his elbow, he watched her dress in soft leather leggings and boots. Still pretending his comments hadn't prodded her along, none of her movements were rushed. Yet she didn't linger, either.

Efficiently she broke camp. Much more efficiently than she had during the first days of the tournament. She had only a few possessions to gather—so different from the woman Strax had met six months before, in a coliseum in Aremond where the race had begun. He and his brother had been standing among three dozen other warriors when a noblewoman had ridden into the stadium on her fine Glacian gelding, leading another horse loaded down with supplies. Her black hair was woven into a shining coronet, and her soft body was clad in silks threaded with gold.

She was the most beautiful woman Strax had ever seen. And he'd assumed her presence in the coliseum meant she must be the victor's prize—and in that moment, he'd wanted to join the tournament in truth so that he could win her. Then he'd discovered she was another contestant.

Strax hadn't expected her to last a week. And he'd told her so.

Yet she'd proven him wrong. After a morning when she'd spent more time packing her camp than traveling, she'd given her extra supplies and horse to a villager she encountered on the side of the road. She'd traded in her fine gelding for a sturdy mare that could better handle the grueling pace. Everything that slowed her, she left behind. Now here she was. No longer as soft—and no longer in silks, but leather and furs.

And still the most beautiful woman he'd ever beheld. So Strax beheld her as often as he could.

Only a few minutes passed before Mara mounted her mare and started down the road at a brisk clip. Strax remained where he was. At some point today, he would make a show of attempting to overtake her. But being in last place suited him. He was not here to win.

So it mattered little if he tarried in bed, stroking the thick length of his cock and picturing the smiling curve of Mara's lush lips. He'd seen her smile before, though it had never been aimed at him. Instead she'd bestowed it upon his twin during those first weeks of the race. But Strax could not be jealous, because everyone smiled at Aruk. Strax's brother was everything that he was not—always laughing and joking, putting both friends and strangers at ease.

And unlike Strax, Aruk was not last; instead he was simply lost.

Strax's throat tightened and a dark ache bloomed in his chest. Determinedly he focused on Mara's lips again—and the memory of her body against his.

He knew that, as well. While crossing the Illwind Sea, a squall had nearly capsized the merchant ship carrying Strax, Aruk, and Mara to the northern shore. After a wave tore Aruk's hand from Strax's grip, carrying his brother into the thrashing waters, Strax had lashed a rope around Mara's waist and tied the other end around his. Then he'd held on to the mast, and from sunset to dawn, she'd clung to him as wave after wave crashed over the decks.

When the storm was finally spent, they'd been battered and wet and cold, yet Strax could still feel the comfort of Mara's hand upon his cheek. He could hear the warmth of her voice in grief and sorrow—and picture the sympathy in her eyes when he'd insisted that Aruk had survived and so he had nothing to grieve.

Just as he did not grieve the way the warmth in her gaze became an angry fire again when he'd stated that, if not for him, she would have drowned that night. That the race was too dangerous for a woman who wasn't a warrior and that she ought to give up and return home. When he'd said she would never win.

But the storm had not been the only night he'd known the softness of her body against his. There had also been the six nights through the Noredge pass, when the bitter cold that fell over the mountains would have killed them in their sleep—except they shared blankets and warmth and a fire. For six nights he'd barely slept, holding Mara's slumbering form tight, his cock and his heart aching for more.

Strax imagined more now, as he had every day since. He imagined that instead of lying stiffly with her back against his chest until her body relaxed into sleep, she had turned to face him. That she'd cradled his face in her hands and drew his mouth to hers. That he'd tasted the heat of her kiss and the sweetness of her cunt before plunging his cock deep. That she'd cried out his name with every powerful thrust, until she began shuddering beneath him, her luscious sheath clasping him tight as he found his own release. That he'd spilled his seed into her clenching depths and not into his hand.

And Strax imagined that afterward, he would not feel this great emptiness within. Instead he would hold her, and every word he said would be the words Strax wished to say—and not the words his duty demanded.

But that could not be. So Strax rose from his furs,

washed the spend from his hand, and checked the snares he'd set the night before. Only two rabbits, yet that would feed him well—and Mara, too, if she failed to catch anything of her own this day. She would glower at him when he tossed the rabbit into her pot and remarked upon her poor hunting skills, yet she never refused the meat. She was proud and stubborn but not foolish.

Strax was a fool for helping her at all. But feeding her also gave him reason to visit her camp, where Mara might ask him to stay and share the meal or invite him to her bed, so a fool he would continue to be.

A slow fool, this morning. Despite his promise to overtake Mara, he let his mount amble at a comfortable pace through the forest road. The tournament map given to each contestant showed that he would soon come upon a crossroads marked by two stone obelisks. The sun was high overhead when he emerged from the woods and saw the obelisks standing upon a grassy mound ahead.

The forest road continued east to Wintermere and the Silver Coast, and was well-traveled. The tournament route continued north, onto a road that was a rough track no wider than a game trail.

Strax guided his horse onto the track—then reined the animal to a halt. The skin on the back of his neck tightened.

There was a powerful enchantment here. The corrupted magic skittered over his senses like a spider bursting with venom. He could feel its presence, but because of the wards inked into his skin, the spell could not affect him.

Mara had no similar protection.

His stomach roiling as if he were in the midst of another storm, upon another ship that might capsize and drag him under, Strax dismounted. The source of the spell he found quickly enough—a lure and an illusion, the runes carved into stones and faintly glowing. A spell that would have made her see or hear something that would have drawn her in. A baby crying, perhaps. Or someone she loved shouting for help.

Quickly he destroyed the spell and began searching for her trail. She had not continued up the northern track; there were no new hoofprints to follow.

Strax raced for the east road. There was sign of Mara here…but not only of Mara. She had been ambushed by three men. And she'd fought—Strax found her bloodied sword wedged into a clump of grass—but lost. Then she'd been taken down the east road.

Attacked. Abducted. And he had not been here to help her.

His blood obligation demanded that he not help her now. Yet he did not even hesitate before leaping into his saddle and galloping down the east road.

Strax had already lost his brother. He would not lose Mara, too.

⁕ ⁕ ⁕

HE TRACKED MARA TO WINTERMERE, and amid the busy streets he lost her trail. But in a city, there were always open eyes to see everything that occurred. The difficulty lay in opening mouths.

Strax had been in kingdoms like Wintermere before. Realms where the citizens looked at him with wary, fearful gazes. Not only because of his size or the sword he carried, but because their courage had been starved and beaten out of them. Aremond, where the tournament had begun and where Mara was from, was such a realm. And in such places, Strax's coins did more to open mouths than the threat of his sword would…but he was willing to use both if necessary.

It didn't prove to be. By the end of the day, he learned of an auction house where a foreign noblewoman was rumored to have been taken. With his last gold coin, Strax bribed the captain of the auction house's guard, claiming he wished to view the merchandise before making his bid. The ease of the transaction told Strax the captain often accepted such bribes. And indeed, they had barely entered the holding pens before the captain slyly suggested that, for the price of another coin, Strax might do more to the caged men and women than view them.

Despite the rage burning in his veins, Strax did not yet draw his sword. Instead his heart thundered as they passed every cage, until he reached the final holding pen. Relief poured through him. Mara was here. Curled on a pallet against the far wall, naked but for the covering of her long hair. Even with her back to them, he knew at a glance it was she. His throat knotted with sheer emotion. Lifting his chin, he indicated to the captain that this was the woman he wished to examine more closely.

"Eyes open and on your feet, wench!" The clang of a brass cudgel against the iron bars followed the captain's command. "A suitor is here to admire you."

Mara didn't stir, but replied in the melodic accent common to the realms south of the Illwind Sea. "Then he can admire my ass, because I have no intention of posing for two-legged swine."

"She believes herself too good to follow orders, which is why she's got Thadus's collar around her throat," the captain said to Strax before raising his voice. "Wench! On your feet, or you'll be slopped with a bucket of piss."

That was hardly a threat to a woman such as Mara. In the months since the Great Tournament had begun, she had suffered worse while overcoming the obstacles along the route. She had dived into a lake of putrid troll slime. She had crawled through a dragon's rotting corpse. She had swallowed a baleworm's fiery spend. Through countless challenges, she had suffered indignities greater than a bucket could ever hold.

And through it all, she had endured. She had fought. And she had prevailed. Even now, she likely plotted her escape from this cage.

Strax had no doubt that she would succeed. But he'd help her succeed more quickly. "Does she enjoy lying abed, then?" Strax asked softly and watched her spine stiffen at the sound of his voice.

The captain laughed. "Better if she does. After the auction, she'll be on her back often enough."

No. But Strax didn't say it aloud, because Mara was getting to her feet, and her sheer beauty stole his every word, his every thought. From her small toes to the lean strength of her thighs, from the silky curls guarding her cunt to the soft handfuls of her breasts. From her full, unsmiling mouth to her dark eyes—

Which did not burn with anger or distrust now. Which did not burn at all. Instead Mara regarded him with a dull, hopeless gaze…as if she were utterly defeated.

Pain ripped through his chest, a hot blade of agonizing grief. Because he'd lost her after all. He'd tarried this morning to stroke his cock, and whatever had happened to her between then and now had doused the fire in her that he loved so desperately. The weight of that loss drowned him, crushing his heart.

"I can't take extra coin for this one." The captain's words sounded muffled, as if Strax heard them underwater. "A virgin fetches a higher price, so she must remain untouched until the auction."

Strax's agony narrowed to a sharp, burning edge. "How are you certain she's untouched?"

"Thadus himself examined her," the other man said, then added with a leer, "'Tis a pity, because me and my guards would have made good use of a beauty like her until—"

Strax slammed the captain's head into the iron bars. The crack of the man's skull and plop of his brains to the ground barely registered over the sound of Mara's indrawn breath. The surprise lighting her gaze was not a fire. But it was a spark, and gladdened Strax so fiercely that he bared his teeth in a grin at the guards rushing him with their swords drawn.

Strax didn't draw his own sword, preferring the satisfaction of his fists. His hands dripped with the blood of a dozen guards when he finally collected the keys from the captain's corpse.

He unlocked Mara's cage and tossed the keys into the next holding pen, where a man stood at the bars staring at him with widened eyes. "Free the others," Strax commanded.

The man rushed to comply. Strax glanced back at Mara. She hadn't made a move toward the open door of her cage. Because of her nudity? He didn't believe that would stop her for even a moment.

Yet he stripped off his own bloodstained tunic and entered her pen. As he pulled the tunic over her bowed head, Mara said in a thick voice, "You needn't have gone to these lengths to overtake me today, warrior."

Frowning, he tipped up her chin. Dull hopelessness still filled her eyes. "Why have you not already freed yourself? You escaped the soul-flayers in Blackpine, yet cannot escape a cage?"

She lifted her chin higher, and his gaze fell to the

delicate wire twisted around her throat. "Because the ruler of this realm is just like Solegius, and has bound me with this collar."

Solegius, the tyrant sorcerer of Aremond. Here in Wintermere, a sorcerer named Thadus sat on the throne.

The same sorcerer who'd examined Mara to see whether she was a virgin. Strax had already planned to kill the man. Now he would kill him much, much more slowly. "What does the collar do?"

"It forces me to obey the orders of any man with a claim on me. For now that man is Thadus, and he ordered me not to leave this cage until I am auctioned. Then the man who buys me will claim me however he wishes to."

Not while Strax lived. And although he knew it would be impossible, he attempted to break the wire. The fragile strand proved stronger than steel.

"I have tried that, warrior," Mara said softly, and he could see that she had. Livid red marked her skin where she had scratched and pulled at the wire. "Only someone with power over the collar can remove it."

Only a man who'd claimed her. Jaw clenched, Strax nodded—and then tossed her slight form up over his shoulder. She couldn't voluntarily leave. So he would carry her out.

Yet the moment he stepped through the door, she began thrashing and choking. Immediately he returned her to the cage, where she gasped for air. A new red mark around her throat showed where the collar had constricted and strangled her.

His own throat feeling as if he'd been garroted, Strax set her down. Voice hoarse, he told her, "I'll return for you."

He didn't know which hurt worse—having to leave Mara alone, or how she clearly didn't believe that he would come back for her.

A sad smile curved her mouth. "Thank you for trying, warrior."

He'd do more than try. Yet saying so would mean nothing to her, because she trusted his words not at all. Only actions mattered now. Silently, Strax pressed a dagger into her hand, so that she could defend herself while he was gone. When he returned, she would never need to protect herself again.

But the dagger was not all Strax gave her. Because Mara might not know it, but his torn and bloodied heart also lay in her hands. And he would never again be free unless she was.

Which meant Strax must kill a king.

MARA
the
DEFEATED

Wintermere

I CANNOT GIVE UP NOW. I CANNOT GIVE UP NOW. I CANNOT give up now.

The five words were a chant in Mara's head, echoed by the silent movement of her lips. If she had been a sorcerer, those words might have had more power. But she was only a woman with no power except for her courage and her will.

Courage and will had gotten her this far, however. So they would also get her out of this cage. She only needed to imagine a way to escape.

In the past six months, Mara had overcome every

obstacle in her path. She could now, too, though her current imprisonment was not part of the tournament. At the crossroads, when she'd heard her mother calling for help, then her younger brothers and sisters screaming, Mara had believed it was yet another danger for the contestants to battle. But it was only a trap, set by a sorcerer tyrant who filled his treasury by trading in human flesh.

The collar circling her neck was cold to the touch, yet still seemed to burn her skin. Had it been a shackle around her wrist, she would have used Strax's dagger to cut off her hand. But cutting off her own head wasn't so easy.

More likely, she'd need to cut off someone else's head. Because the more she considered her options, it seemed only one remained. The collar would force her to submit to an auction and to endure whatever horrors befell her afterward. So her only choice was to bide her time, wait for an opportunity to kill the man who bought her, and then escape.

But time was the one thing Mara did not have. If another contestant returned to Aremond with the gauntlet and won the tournament, everyone Mara had ever known and loved would die.

So she could not give up now. No matter how tired and lonely she was. No matter how her heart ached with despair and fear.

It ached more fiercely since Strax had left her. She had no hope he would return. In truth, she wasn't certain he'd really come.

When Mara first heard his voice speaking to the captain of the guard, she'd believed she was dreaming—or was in a nightmare. For six months, Strax had been the bane of her existence. The barbarian rarely opened his mouth, yet whenever he did, it was only to insult her. To say that she was not clever enough or strong enough to win the tournament. That she was not fast enough.

And he was not wrong. Every other warrior competing in this tournament was far ahead. All but one. Almost from the beginning, Strax had trailed her. Sometimes within sight, sometimes a day or two behind. But always following. And despite his insults, Mara had comforted herself with the knowledge that she wasn't in last place.

But that was no longer true. When she'd been captured, the misery of being caged and collared had been enough to bear. That the barbarian wasn't here to witness her humiliation and defeat had been her only consolation.

Then he'd come. Yet to her astonishment, the barbarian hadn't humiliated her or insulted her further. And if she hadn't been clutching his dagger in her hand, she'd have believed his appearance was yet another sorcerer's illusion—a spell designed to show her the Strax that she'd always wished he would be. A warrior who helped her. A warrior who so gently touched her face. A warrior who looked at her with concern and warmth instead of doubt and disdain.

If his presence had been a spell, it would have been a cruel illusion, indeed. To have Strax suddenly be everything she wished he was…and then watch him leave.

But Mara could not blame Strax for going. Only powerful magic could defeat this collar. Why would he risk everything—the tournament or his life—to save a woman he always mocked?

Of course he would not. So Strax had abandoned Mara here with a confusing mix of gratitude and despair roiling within her heart…and a dagger that she might soon need to use.

All of the other prisoners had fled the auction house. For almost an hour, Mara's only company had been the bloodied corpses outside her cell. Yet she could hear someone approaching now—and her cage door was unlocked, offering her no protection.

Her grip tightened on the dagger. Heart pounding, she debated whether to hide, curling herself out of sight in the corner of her cage.

But Mara had never been one to run and hide. So she stood in the middle of her cell, eyes narrowed down the length of the dim passageway.

For a moment, she didn't recognize the enormous figure who came out of the shadows. And when she did recognize him, it took another moment to believe he was there.

Strax.

As she'd never seen him before, nearly every inch of his skin painted crimson with blood. He'd always been a huge, barbaric figure, his black hair carelessly tied back in a strip of leather. Now the strands hung around his face, dripping with gore. And she'd seen him many times without a tunic—he hadn't even begun wearing one until the weather grew so cold that ice covered the puddles in the road each morning—yet he'd never appeared so terrifyingly strong, his sinewy muscles like sculpted granite and his stride the smooth prowl of a panther's, gripping his sword in one hand and a man's head in the other.

With dropped jaw, she watched him toss the head into her piss bucket…but not before she saw the death-slackened face. That head belonged to the ruler of Wintermere—Thadus the sorcerer, whose collar circled her neck, and who'd forced her legs open to confirm her virginity.

She'd wished Thadus dead then. But he'd been surrounded by guards and resided in the fortress at the center of the city—and with a few words, his magic could have killed her.

Now his head was in her bucket, and Mara was only sorry that she hadn't yet shit in it.

And she was astonished. That head meant Strax must have fought his way into the fortress. He must have defeated Thadus's guards, before defeating the sorcerer himself…and he must have done it alone. She could hardly comprehend the skill and power the barbarian must have. Never had he shown it before. Such a warrior shouldn't have been in last place in any tournament. He should have been leading the pack.

Yet he'd trailed behind them all. Why?

She tipped her head back, keeping her gaze on Strax's face as he came nearer. Never had he seemed so big…yet he was also never so close. His bloodied fingers tipped her chin higher.

A frown darkened his features when he still could not break the collar's thin wire. "The sorcerer would not remove the spell or give me claim over you," he said in the deep, guttural accent of the Dead Lands. How a barren wasteland grew such powerful warriors, Mara didn't know. Yet both he and his twin brother were larger and stronger than any other warriors who had joined the tournament.

"So you killed him?" Because a spell often died with a sorcerer. But this spell had not.

"This magic resides in the collar. So I must claim you before I can break it."

"Do you have enough gold to buy me at the auction, warrior?" Mara might have had enough, but her purse had been taken by the villains who'd ambushed her, along with her horse. She had nothing now but her tunic and dagger—both of which Strax had given her.

"There is not enough gold in the world to buy a woman of your worth." His jaw hardened and his fingers slipped from her neck, yet she could still feel the sticky warmth of the bloodied marks he left. "I will return again."

She stared after him. This *must* be an illusion of some sort. Or a trick. A woman of her worth? Mara could not count the number of times he'd implied she was worthless.

So this time she believed he would return…yet she

was also wary. Because she didn't understand him at all—or this attempt to free her. What purpose could it have? Not to help her. Because in six months, he hadn't helped her. He'd only said over and over again that she was bound to fail. So she couldn't trust that he truly meant to help her now.

At midnight, Strax returned—no longer covered in blood, and no longer alone. Accompanying him was a thin, bald man in dark robes and with wide, terrified eyes.

Strax shoved the trembling man into the cage. "This magistrate can marry us."

Had the barbarian gone completely mad? Strax's eyes seemed to burn with an unholy, feverish fire as they settled on Mara, and that look sent shivers racing over her skin.

Certain she'd misunderstood, Mara shook her head. "You want him to *marry* us?"

"A husband has a claim on his wife. No magic can deny that."

Mara couldn't refute that truth, yet still…why would he do this? It made no sense at all. Her chest tight, she told him, "You understand, warrior, that I am from Aremond. I am not from a kingdom such as Savadon or Galoth, where they marry on a whim and untie their wedding ribbon when marriage no longer suits them. You'll always be bound to me."

That fire in his eyes flared brighter. "And I am from the Dead Lands. A warrior will let nothing separate him from his wife. So *you* will always be bound to *me*."

Heart pounding so hard she was almost dizzy with it, she looked to the magistrate. "You have the red ribbon?"

The man held up a length of crimson silk in his shaking fingers. So they had all that was needed.

Except an explanation. With emotion clogging her throat, Mara met Strax's gaze again. "I will do anything to be free—so I will marry you," she told him, but held up her hand when he stepped forward with a fierce light on his expression. "But I need to know why you are marrying me."

"Because I love you," he said gruffly and Mara wished that she hadn't asked. She would rather be given no answer than be given a lie.

Yet *she* had not lied. She'd do anything to continue her quest to win the gauntlet. Even marry a man she could not trust to tell the truth. Who thought she was weak and stupid and who insulted her at every turn.

With a sickly pain in her heart, Mara stepped closer to Strax and nodded to the magistrate. She raised her hand, and as Strax placed his huge palm against hers, she could hardly bear to look at him.

And she wondered what else he'd lied about. As the magistrate weaved the ribbon between their fingers, she asked, "Do you swear you'll free me from this collar the moment we are married?"

Because as soon as he had a claim on her, Strax's power over her would be absolute. He could order her to do anything and Mara would have to obey. Perhaps his declaration of love was a ruse so that he could control her. Or humiliate her. Or worse.

"I will," he vowed, and the pain in Mara's heart grew. Because she still couldn't trust his word, though she wanted nothing more than to trust it. She wanted to believe in the devotion deepening his voice and the steady darkness of his eyes.

So as the magistrate finished winding the ribbon between their fingers, with her other hand Mara raised her dagger to Strax's muscled throat and pressed the sharpened point into the only soft spot he seemed to have, where a pulse drummed visibly in the thick column of his neck. "After our vows are spoken, if any command issues from your lips except the words to free me, they will be the last you ever utter."

"You think I will order you onto your back and your thighs to spread? Command you to come with every thrust of my cock?" Eyes narrowed, Strax slowly shook his head—not seeming to care that the movement drew drops of blood from where she held the blade against his skin. "I need no magic to make my woman come, Mara. The pleasure I'll give you will be no illusion."

Heat flared beneath her skin at the thought of it. Yet she still couldn't trust that he meant a word. "I want nothing from you except my freedom," she declared hotly—and because Strax had made her a liar now, too, she snapped at the magistrate, "Begin."

The magistrate stammered, "But…we…we…have no

witnesses—"

Strax's foot lashed out. The bucket flew, and Thadus's head bounced against the iron bars before rolling to a stop with empty eyes staring at them and dripping yellow tears. "Your king himself bears witness. *Begin.*"

Fear blanched the magistrate's face. With shaking hands, he lifted the two ends of the ribbon. "Ah, the bride…you are called…?"

"Lady Maraserit ik Terin of Aremond."

After repeating her name, the magistrate asked, "Do you pledge yourself to this man and swear to be his faithful wife?"

"I will," she promised, holding her dagger ready to slit Strax's throat.

"And you…?"

"Strax," he said in a thick voice, "Keeper of the Sacred Oath, son of the Fang Clan of the Dead Lands. I pledge myself to this woman and vow to be her faithful husband."

"Then you are now bound together," the magistrate said, knotting the ends of the ribbon. "Upon a kiss that seals your vows, you will be wife and husband."

Mara didn't move, her right hand tied to his and her left hand holding the blade at his throat. Slowly she relaxed her wrist, allowing Strax to bend his head toward hers—yet never letting even a hair's breadth of space between her dagger and his skin. Her breath trembled wildly as he gently tilted up her chin. His gaze smoldered, dark and hot, and seemed to ignite an answering fire within her.

She shut her eyes but couldn't shut out the pulse thundering in her ears, the gentle pressure of his strong fingers, the warmth of his breath whispering over her lips. Then his firm mouth claimed hers, and that was enough, it should have been enough—even a touch of lips was a kiss, so they were married now. But instead of backing away, Strax pushed closer. His big hand cradled the nape of her neck as he tasted and teased, and when her lips parted it was only to remind him that he would die if he betrayed her. Yet she couldn't speak, because his tongue slicked over hers, and an emotion wild and sweet swept into her with that lick. A hunger for more of this. Not just a kiss but the way Strax made her feel, the way he touched her now. As if he truly did love her.

But how could she believe that? How?

With burning eyes and racing heart, she turned her face from his. But she couldn't pull away. His hand still clasped her nape and the wedding ribbon had to remain tied until dawn. "Free me now," she whispered. "Or I will kill you."

His reply was a harsh rasp against her ear. "You are already free…wife."

In astonishment Mara brought her beribboned fingers to her neck—bringing his bound hand with hers. The collar was gone. She hadn't even felt him remove it during the kiss. Now the horrid thing lay at her feet, nothing but a useless, twisted wire.

Her wondering gaze flew to Strax's face and only

encountered his strong profile as he looked to the magistrate. "You'll find your payment of a gold coin in that dead captain's purse," he said, then Mara gave a startled gasp when the barbarian abruptly spun her around and swept her up to cradle her against his broad chest. "Let us attempt this again."

Leaving the cage. Mara held her breath as he carried her through. But of course the collar could not strangle her…because he'd freed her.

Now her new husband held her while he strode out of the auction house, one steely arm supporting her knees and the other behind her back. Because of their bound hands, there was no point in demanding that he put her down. One of them would have to walk backward; yet he could carry her as long as she held her arm crossed over her chest.

Mara didn't glance at any of the carnage they passed, the bodies of the guards littering the floor. She only looked at Strax. Such a strange, warm hope filled her chest that she couldn't have spoken even if she wished to. He'd come to Wintermere to help her. He'd killed a sorcerer king to save her. And then he'd freed her.

Perhaps he might help her win this tournament, too. And perhaps she could truly trust him.

Never had she wanted anything so much.

Outside, the entire city seemed in uproar. From every direction came the sound of citizens in riot. Because Strax had killed a tyrant. And he'd freed more than Mara in doing so.

Yet he seemed utterly unaffected by the fighting around them. He carried her as if through a spring meadow. And another astonishment awaited Mara when they reached his horse, because tied next to his mount was her mare.

"Where did you find her?" she asked in wonder as he lifted her onto his gelding—which she didn't protest, because they couldn't ride different horses with their hands tied.

"When I tracked down the men who ambushed you." Easily he leapt up behind her, the fingers of their beribboned hand entwined, his arm around her waist. He pulled her back snug against his hard chest, holding her securely. "But aside from your saddle and horse, your belongings were already gone. Do you wish to look for them now?"

For her furs and clothes and gold. "No," Mara said. They would waste valuable time searching—and she hardly needed those things now. Her legs were bare from mid-thigh to toes, yet never had she felt so safe, so warm as with Strax holding her. And it was becoming harder to tell herself that his actions tonight had been a trick of some sort.

Yet nothing about him made sense. Not after what he'd done here. As they rode toward the city gate, one clear answer occurred to her. "You never intended to win the tournament, did you?"

"No," he replied gruffly.

"Are you…a final obstacle? Something the contestants

must overcome after they've retrieved the gauntlet?"

Which would explain why he was in last place. Anyone returning to Aremond would have to pass him—and would have to defeat him.

Would he allow *her* to pass him? He was her husband now. And he'd risked so much to save her. Perhaps he'd help her save everyone else she loved, too.

"I am not an obstacle." His voice deepened. "I am bound by a blood oath to never let a sorcerer such as Solegius of Aremond possess the gauntlet—and I will destroy anyone who attempts to give it to him."

The hope growing in Mara's chest withered into a painful, poisoned lump. A blood oath. If Strax betrayed it, not only would he die…but so would all of his clan.

So she didn't respond. As they rode out of the city, she stared blindly ahead—and all that lived inside her now was misery and despair. Her husband held her in his arms, his warm breath stirred her hair, yet she felt utterly alone again.

Strax must have been more wary in the city than he'd appeared, because once they were away from the chaos, tension eased from the warrior's muscles. Quietly he asked her, "Did you join the tournament to win the prize? If it is gold you seek, my wife, I will find riches for you elsewhere."

"I have riches," she told him, her voice thick with unshed tears. "Solegius imprisoned my family and enslaved everyone under our protection. If I do not return with the gauntlet, he'll kill them all."

Strax stiffened behind her. For an endless time, the barbarian didn't speak. When he finally did, his accent was so deep it sounded as if he choked on every word. "I cannot let you give the gauntlet to him."

His declaration pierced Mara's heart like a dagger. "We must be enemies, then."

"No," Strax denied roughly, his arm tightening and holding her closer. "You are my wife."

"And if you try to stop me from winning, I'll soon be a widow."

"You cannot win—"

"So you return to insults again? I *will* win." No longer unshed, hot tears spilled silently down her cheeks. "Perhaps you don't believe I am capable, warrior, but I've proven you wrong over and over again. I will prove you wrong this time, too. And if you stand in my way, I will kill you."

"I *know* you are capable," he snarled. "But I cannot let… I cannot…" His voice seemed to strangle itself and his hand rose to her face. She tried to turn away, to conceal this from him, yet he found the evidence of her pain.

"Shed more tears, Mara," he said bleakly. "And you will kill me easily."

So he claimed. Yet Strax seemed strong enough as her tears continued to fall, holding her so tightly that she could almost believe he was a warrior who would help her, protect her…love her.

It was only another illusion. A dream that would

disappear at dawn. But for a little while, Mara allowed herself to dream that he was everything she'd ever wanted him to be. And she dreamt it until she fell asleep in his arms.

STRAX
the
VOWKEEPER

The Road

Strax had married Mara at midnight. By dawn, his bride was already trying to run away.

And she was trying to do it quietly. She'd fallen asleep in his arms while they rode away from Wintermere, then briefly awakened again when he made camp. Custom demanded their hands remain tied with the red ribbon until morning, so she hadn't protested when he'd made a single bed, nor when he'd determined that the easiest position for them to sleep was with Strax on his back and Mara lying atop his chest. There she'd fallen quickly asleep again, her head pillowed on his shoulder and her legs straddling his waist, while Strax had lain beneath her with his cock hard and his heart full.

So very full—because Mara was his wife. And despite her anger and distrust, she must feel safe with him to fall asleep in his arms so easily. And his heart was full because she had wept upon discovering that he must stop her from returning the gauntlet to her tyrant king. Her every tear had pierced Strax's chest…yet his wife had shed those tears because she believed they must be enemies. If the thought disappointed and hurt her, Mara must want more from Strax than she had ever said.

Strax didn't know the solution to the chasm that yawned between them. He would discover a way to bridge it, though. Because he would never be separated from his wife.

But she was already putting distance between them. Ever so slowly, only moving her fingers, she began to work her hand free of the ribbon. Not a sound she made, as if she feared waking him. Her warm breath trembled softly against his neck. The softness of her breasts pressed into his chest, with only her tunic to prevent her skin from touching his. Yet nothing lay between her inner thighs clasping his sides or the sultry warmth of her woman-hood from his stomach. She'd been naked in that cell when he'd given her his tunic to wear and she was still bare beneath it.

The ribbon's knot loosened, freeing her hand from his—yet Strax could not let her go. When his fingers clasped hers, telling her that he was awake, her body went utterly still.

Utterly still and waiting…because although Mara felt safe enough to sleep in his arms, she also didn't trust him. His heart ached with the knowing of it—and knowing that he'd done nothing to earn her trust in all these months.

But Strax would begin to earn it on this day. He would earn her trust and anything else she'd be willing to give him.

"Forgive me, Mara," he said to her softly.

Silence reigned for a breath, as if she couldn't think of a reason why he needed to be forgiven. Finally she whispered, "What for?"

"Because I didn't wake you in the manner a husband should wake his wife."

"What manner is that?"

Strax would have preferred to show her. Instead he told her, "With my head between your thighs and my mouth upon your cunt."

Her breath stopped against his throat. Convulsively her fingers tightened on his. Yet she said not a word.

Hunger roughened his voice. "Do you wish me to wake you properly, my wife?"

Her hesitation made his heart soar. The abrupt "No!" that followed mattered not at all, because that brief hesitation exposed the temptation she must feel—as did her body when, in the rush of getting away from him, she rocked back to sit up and her femininity encountered the turgid cockstand that jutted up over his lower abdomen.

She froze, and in the dim light, Strax saw the way her gaze widened and her lips parted. But all he could feel was her feminine flesh—so hot and wet against his bare shaft—and groan when she bit her lower lip and hitched her hips down, then up and up and up, as if measuring the rigid length of him with the slick heat of her cunt. Her body shuddered when she reached the tip and the blunt head of his cock rolled over her clitoris. A soft moan escaped her throat and her eyes rolled back, then all at once she was on her feet, the furs thrown aside and frigid air kissing the trail of wetness she'd left behind on his erection.

Even as Strax clenched his jaw against the agonizing arousal that she'd mercilessly abandoned, joy burst through him. So blessed he was, to have a wife as hot as the sun and as wet as the ocean. All such a woman needed was a man as solid as the earth itself—and that was he. Strax would be the firm ground beneath her feet and the hard stone that filled her cunt.

He rolled onto his side, gripping his cock to stroke her honeyed wetness into his skin. Mara was already preparing to leave, carrying her saddle to her horse. A frown pulled at his mouth as he watched her cross the harsh, cold ground in her bare feet.

"Take my boots, wife. And my leather leggings, too." They would be far too big for her, just as his tunic was, but she could lace them tight enough to stay on. In the chill spring air, he could make do by tying a fur around his waist.

"Stuff your boots up your ass," she snapped and Strax grinned. "And lie abed all morning as you usually do, *husband.*"

The word was a sneer. In a lithe movement, she mounted her mare—then abruptly stopped when her gaze fell upon him, her mouth open as if she'd meant to say something else but the sight of Strax running his big fist the length of his cock knocked the words from her tongue.

"This is why I always lie abed, Mara," he told her gruffly while his fingers squeezed and stroked his throbbing erection. "I remain in my furs and dream of having you."

Her startled gaze flew from his cock to his face, and doubt filled her voice. "You dreamt of me? But you always said…you would say that I was…"

She trailed off, her throat working. Almost reluctantly it seemed, she glanced at his thick length again. A deep breath lifted her breasts within his tunic, her stiffened nipples showing faintly through the heavy weave. The tip of her tongue darted out to touch the upper bow of her lip as a pearled drop of seed spilled from the crown.

Then without another word, she reined her horse around and started off—not along the road west, but striking out to the north.

Before this day, Strax would have lingered in his furs until his seed spurted into his hand. But yesterday he'd done so and she'd been captured. Imprisoned. And the fire that burned inside her had almost been doused.

Now it flamed brightly again…and Strax would follow that flame, wherever she went. He had two vows to keep—one a blood oath to never allow the gauntlet's power to be abused, and the other a promise to be her devoted husband.

Somehow, he would fulfill both vows. But he could not do that abed.

So with his cock still throbbing, Strax leapt to his feet and followed her.

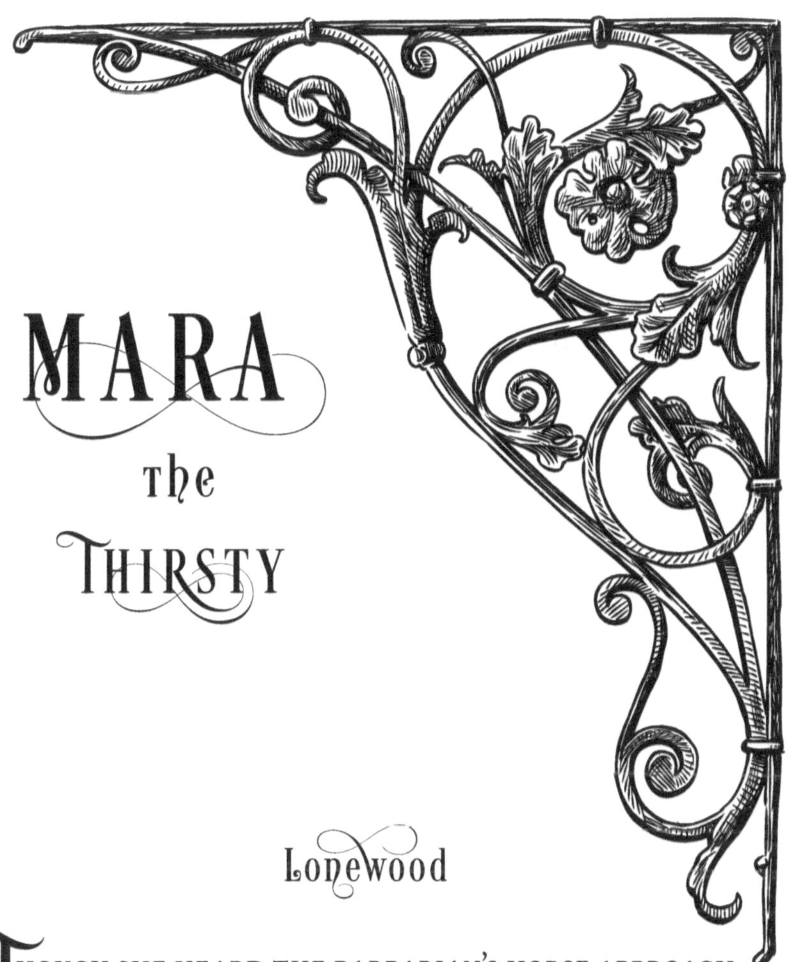

MARA

the

THIRSTY

Lonewood

Though she heard the barbarian's horse approach-ing, Mara refused to look back. Instead she kept her gaze focused ahead. In the distance, the black eye sockets of the Skull Cliffs stared out over the plains. Legend was that the skulls belonged to the cruel gods who'd once roamed this land, before the goddess Khides had slain them and put their giant rotting heads on display as a warning to any other being who might abuse others with his power.

If the legend had any truth to it, Mara didn't know. She only knew that the cliffs were the final obstacle before she reached Khides' keep. All that lay between her and those cliffs was several days' journey across the Lonewood plain…and a husband who intended to stop her from winning the tournament.

The only pain greater than knowing Strax was bound by a blood oath to stop her was the pain of imagining what would happen to her family if she failed. Her brothers and sisters—the youngest of whom was only five years of age. Her parents, who'd only shown love and kindness to all who'd sought help from them during Solegius's cruel reign. Their only crime had been standing firm against the sorcerer king's tyranny…and for refusing to send Mara to his bed.

She'd gone anyway when Solegius threatened to retaliate against her family for their defiance. Then she'd committed the unforgivable crime that sealed everyone's fate.

When Solegius had lowered his handsome face to kiss her, she'd gagged.

Her punishment for that insult to his vanity was to make her join a tournament no one believed she could survive, let alone win. But sending her on a route that should kill her was not enough for Solegius, so he'd added the burden of thousands of lives upon her shoulders.

Mara would be carrying that burden up those cliffs, just as she'd carried it across thousands of miles. That weight hadn't broken her as everyone expected; instead it had strengthened her.

Yet no matter how strong she'd become, Mara still struggled to shrug off Strax's insults and doubts. Nor could she easily shrug away the hurt of knowing he could never help her win the tournament. But even if he wasn't obligated by a blood vow to stop her, she couldn't depend on him. So their marriage had changed nothing.

Except now she knew why he'd always followed in last place. He didn't stay behind her this day, however, instead riding up alongside her mare and matching her pace.

"Fill your belly, wife," he commanded, holding out a thick slice of bread topped with soft white cheese and golden honey.

Her stomach rumbled at the sight—and since everything she owned had been stolen except for her sword and a few items in her saddlebags, Mara accepted the meal. Her soft thanks was met with a look of such fierce satisfaction that she didn't glance at him again while she ate. Nonetheless, Mara was acutely aware of his huge presence beside her. Her husband wore the leathers and boots she'd refused, yet despite the cold drizzle that fell from gray skies, he didn't drape his furs over his shoulders and chest. Instead Strax faced the rain as a mountain did, with water running in rivulets over the stony ridges of his muscles, silently inviting her to quench her thirst by sipping from the streams that flowed over his bronze skin.

Oh, and she was *so* very thirsty.

She licked her sticky lips and looked over to find Strax staring at her mouth, his eyes hot enough to catch her blood afire.

"I will see you well fed, Mara," he said in a voice thick

with desire, a voice that promised to fill her up with more than bread.

A voice that touched every yearning need inside her. Not just the thirst of her tongue, or even of the hunger of her body, but the painful longing within her heart. Because she was tired and lonely, and this journey had been so very hard. The only pleasure she'd known since leaving home had been the pleasure Strax had given since freeing her from that cage. His slow, thorough kiss when he'd married her. The warmth and strength of his arms holding her so tight. The fierce, burning sensation of his bare skin against hers, and the sheer ecstasy of feeling his rigid length against her most intimate flesh.

Strax had killed a tyrant to save her. And she hated the hope that rose within her now, like a foolish rabbit leaving the safety of its underground burrow, despite knowing that disappointment waited to pounce and tear it to shreds. "You destroyed Thadus. Could you not do the same to Solegius?"

Jaw clenching, Strax shook his head. "Thadus was unprepared for the likes of me. Solegius is not."

"The likes of you?"

He indicated his side, where runes carved over his ribs glowed faintly gold and protected him against enchantments and spells. Mara only knew what purpose the runes served because his brother Aruk had once told her. Everyone in the Dead Lands was born with more power than any sorcerer in the west—yet they almost all voluntarily bound their magic to their own flesh with those runes, rendering themselves incapable of casting spells except for the protective wards written into their skin. Aruk had called a sorcerer's spells corrupted magic that slowly pushed the world out of balance. And he'd claimed that love and kindness were pure, uncorrupted magic—and the most powerful of all magics—followed by courage and trust, and rage and hate.

The love Mara felt for her family seemed enough to fill an ocean. So did her hate for Solegius. Yet neither her love nor hate could save them and defeat Aremond's king, no matter what the barbarians in the Dead Lands believed.

"Thadus attacked me with spells," Strax continued. "But he'd have been better served to enchant a weapon and use it against me. Solegius knows that. If he hadn't protected himself so well, Aruk and I would have killed him when we were in Aremond."

Impervious to spells, but not against items enchanted by spells. "Would Thadus's collar have bound you as it did me?"

"It would."

Strax hadn't been able to break the collar, either. As she recalled what else Strax told her before he'd removed it, the sweet honey on her tongue turned bitter. "I suppose your love is what broke the enchantment on the collar."

"It is," he agreed easily.

Her throat tightened. "Why do you lie? You claimed me. That gave you power over the collar. That is all."

His steady gaze met hers. "And what led me to claim you? Why did I follow you, if not because I love you?"

The pain of hearing it again was like a knife in her chest. "Stop," she begged him, hating both the plea and how the thickness of her voice betrayed her hurt. "I cannot bear you saying that to me."

Not when she knew it to be untrue. Perhaps he lusted after her or pitied her. She could accept that those reasons drove him to Wintermere. But love? No.

She might wish it, but wishing had no more magic than love or trust did. No matter what he said.

Torment darkened his eyes—a torment she'd seen in him before, on the night his brother had been swept overboard into an unforgiving sea. Unable to bear the pain in that look, Mara glanced away from him, but his hoarse reply followed her. "Until you trust my word, I will not say it again. Never would I hurt you, Mara."

That she damn well *knew* for a lie. These past six months, he'd hurt her with his words again and again. Every time he'd told her to give up. Every time he hadn't believed in her.

Her husband didn't think she could win. So she didn't understand why he rode at her side now.

"If someone has already claimed the gauntlet," she told him tightly, "then you are on the wrong road to intercept them."

They were not on a road at all, but striking a new path north from Wintermere to the cliffs. But her observation seemed not to concern Strax.

With a shrug, he told her, "If the gauntlet is gone when we reach the keep, I'll pursue whoever took it and stop him before he reaches Aremond. But the gauntlet will still be there."

How could he be so certain? "More than thirty warriors are ahead of me."

"And in the countless generations since the gauntlet was locked inside the keep, thousands more have attempted to take it—and they all failed. Do you believe such a powerful weapon would be left undefended?"

"Weapon?" She looked to him in confusion. "It is but a useless artifact."

Strax shook his head. "That is a lie spread by my clan to prevent others from seeking its power. Yet Solegius must have learned the truth."

Sending warriors to fetch the gauntlet for him and calling it a tournament? "Why would he not seek it himself?"

"Because a sorcerer's corrupted magic is useless within Khides' keep. And Solegius is nothing without his spells and enchantments."

That was truth. Yet Mara could hardly grasp the rest… though it also made sense. Why would any warrior swear a blood oath over a useless artifact? No one would. "What kind of weapon is it?"

"It's one of two gauntlets that the goddess Khides forged from the hearts of the gods she killed." He gestured ahead at the Skull Cliffs. His tone deepened and became more rhythmic, as if this was a story often heard or often told. "When her own life began to fade, Khides passed the gauntlets to a queen she trusted, who in turn passed them on to her twin sons. Together the brothers ruled, until one of the gauntlets was destroyed while they battled the demon hordes, and they began to fight for possession of the remaining one. Because despite the love they had for each other, neither brother trusted that the other would wield the gauntlet's power as it should be wielded."

The demon hordes? That was a time not simply ancient, but so far in the past that all Mara knew of that age were legends of legends. "You are speaking of the wolf brothers who broke the world. That is only a tale parents tell their children to make them stop arguing."

"It is not a tale," Strax said. "And they were not wolves, but kings who broke the world. But with the last of her strength, Khides joined the pieces together, and built her stone keep—and made the brothers' descendants vow that they would stop anyone from misusing the gauntlet's power again."

"Those descendants became your clan?"

Face grim, he nodded. "And my brother and I are the last."

Are the last. Because he still believed that his brother lived. "Why does your clan not reside at the keep?"

"The gauntlet's guardians do. The blood oath only demands that we do not allow anyone to misuse the weapon—and who could be trusted to wield so much power? Not Solegius." His dark eyes met hers. "If you put the gauntlet into that sorcerer's hands, not only your family or your people will be killed and enslaved. Solegius would enslave the world. So even if I were not bound by a blood oath, I'd do everything I could to prevent him from possessing it. Would you not do the same if you were me?"

A deep ache opened up in her heart. Because she *would* do the same. But she was not him. In a painful whisper, Mara said, "If you wish to fulfill your oath, you should ride the other road. Perhaps no one else has retrieved the gauntlet, but you can't be certain. Yet you are certain I have not."

"I will not leave your side, wife. Nor will you want me to."

Something in his voice stopped her automatic denial. She glanced over with a frown.

Strax gestured ahead. "That is Lonewood's tree."

The cursed tree that sucked the surrounding land dry, leaving only a barren wasteland. Its crooked trunk was clearly visible in the distance, and although they were still passing through the grasslands north of Wintermere, the vegetation around them had been steadily thinning, as if they approached Lonewood's border.

"I had thought it farther from the city," Mara said. And she'd thought it would be taller, too. It had always been described as such.

"The tree is two day's ride from here, and the wasteland stretches two days beyond that."

Her eyes widened. Two days away? Then it must truly be enormous. She could not begin to fathom its height… yet she began to fathom why Strax had said she wouldn't want him to leave her side.

He spoke the reason succinctly. "That is four days of no game to hunt, no water to drink, and no feed for the horses."

Except for the supplies he carried with him, Mara realized. All that remained in her saddlebags were a few packets of dried herbs and a single gold coin that had been wedged into a loose seam.

That coin could buy all the supplies Mara needed…if she returned to Wintermere. Yet no amount of gold could buy what she needed more than anything else: time. She would lose at least a full day in Wintermere, if not more.

She couldn't afford to waste that time. "You asked what I would do if I were you. But what if your family could only be saved by putting the gauntlet into his hands?"

"I would do the same as you are, Mara," he said softly.

She wished that answer eased the ache in her heart but it only made her want to weep. "Instead you will prevent me from saving them."

"I will only prevent you from taking the gauntlet to Aremond. But I would help you save them another way."

"What way?" she cried in frustration. "Do you think we in Aremond have not tried to defeat Solegius? He destroys every army that marches against him. So how will we save my family?"

Her husband had no answer to that. And the only way that Mara could see…Strax would try to stop her. So she would stop him first.

STRAX

the

HUNGRY

Lonewood

H IS WIFE WAS UP TO SOMETHING.

The quiet that fell over Mara as she traveled was not so unusual, though the looks she gave him now were different. No longer were they filled with so much anger or distrust. Strax might have rejoiced over that, except the sadness darkening her gaze when it lingered on him and the depth of the silence between them seemed like a yawning chasm that he could not cross. He stayed closer to her side than he had in six months of journeying, yet she seemed further from him than ever before…and Strax sensed that she was moving even further away with every step forward.

Yet when night fell, she didn't insist on sleeping apart, as Strax expected. Perhaps it was her sensible mind recognizing they only had furs enough for one bed. She also said nothing when, as he always did, Strax stripped to his skin before settling under the covers. Yet she didn't encourage him, either, offering him neither touches nor kisses; wearing her tunic, she meekly lay down beside him. When he rolled onto his side and pulled her back against his chest, she went compliantly. Then she pillowed her head on his biceps and slept.

Strax did not. Instead he wondered what she planned. Because Mara was never compliant or meek. So every moment he expected her to slip from his arms. Or bash his head with a rock. She had wanted Strax to take another road and to be away from him. He doubted that she'd given up on her wish.

His Mara never gave up on anything.

In the darkest hours, slumber finally pulled at him. It seemed he'd only closed his eyes when dawn's golden light opened them again, and he found Mara had turned in his arms and was looking up at him with an expression of sheer determination.

So now she would bash his head, Strax thought. And he would let her. Then he would find her again.

Instead she whispered, "Will you wake me as a husband should wake his wife?"

Raw lust ripped through his senses. His morning

erection hardened into burning steel in the space of the breath it took to roll Mara onto her back and cover her mouth with his. She stiffened for the barest moment, as if not expecting a kiss—he'd only said that a husband woke his wife with his mouth between her legs—then she melted beneath him, her fingers diving into his hair, her tongue hungrily seeking his. Her thighs parted to make room for him, her tunic riding up over her hips, and they both groaned when the thick ridge of his cock wedged against her feminine center.

Scorching wetness burned the length of his shaft and slicked the insides of her thighs. So aroused was she, his wife was drowning in her need. Almost in pain she seemed, writhing helplessly against him, seeking more pleasure and her release.

Strax would give her both, then return to her mouth to give her more. Never had a journey been so beautiful nor as sweet as the path from her lush lips to her curving hips. This time he flew over it, yet the next time, he vowed that his mouth and hands would worship her body as she deserved. But first he would wake her as a husband should.

Ravenous with hunger, Strax pushed her thighs wide and bowed his head, breathing in the heady scent of her arousal.

And now he knew her plan. The faintest perfume of cherries mingled with her own luscious fragrance. Barely detectable, yet distinct. She had bathed her cunt in bellewood blossom.

When the blossoms were steeped, they became a powerful sleeping potion. Yet if the stems were also steeped, a fatal poison was made. And it was impossible to know by scent which it was.

What would she give him? Potion or poison?

Strax didn't think it would be poison. She'd threatened to kill him if he stopped her from retrieving the gauntlet—and he'd told her over and over again that he intended to. But if his Mara meant to kill him, he didn't think it would be in this sly way. No, she would come directly at him with a blade.

From between her thighs, he glanced up. Mara had risen onto her elbows, her lips swollen and reddened by his kisses, her skin flushed with desire, her hair in a wild tangle as she watched him. Her request had been a trick so that she could drug him, yet the passion he saw now wasn't false. Nor was the honeyed arousal that glistened so near to his mouth.

She was so clever, his wife. And so beautiful. Her breath hitched when he parted her with his thumbs. "Will it be death, Mara?" he asked her, his voice harsh with need. "Or only sleep?"

Her body stilled. Her eyes widened, and he recognized the sudden fear there—as if she thought he might punish her for this attempt.

He gripped her hip to prevent her from fleeing, pressed a soothing kiss to the soft skin above her curls. "Do you not know that I would risk death for a taste of you? That

I would happily die if it brought you pleasure?"

And he did, with a long slow lick that tasted of cherries and of Mara's own sweet honey. Her strangled gasp of surprise deepened into a moan when he licked away the remainder of the bellewood blossom from the lips of her cunt, then delved between her folds to find the flavor that was hers alone. He only wanted Mara upon his tongue as he made her come.

But he would not have long to do it. Already a foreign heaviness was settling into his limbs. He knew not whether it was sleep or death that approached, and only cared that he pleased her before it took him.

With a swirl of his tongue, he circled her clit before closing his lips around that sensitive bud. She cried out when he began to suck, her hands fisting in his hair, her back arching. The sound of his name from her panting lips was even sweeter than her cunt. Unable to resist, he abandoned her clitoris for a deep thrusting lick past her virgin entrance, yet she wordlessly begged for more, lifting her hips as if seeking what he hadn't yet given.

Strax would give her all he could. His mouth returned to her clit even as he filled her cunt with the blunt thickness of his longest finger, working it slowly into her snug channel. So tight and hot was his wife that every inch he gained became a victory, and his head swam with the ecstasy of her taste. Then abruptly her voluptuous inner walls clamped down, squeezing his finger so hard that seed spilled from his cock in response.

Her soft flesh muffled his tortured groan. Slowly he began to fuck her with the gentle pumping of his hand as he feasted on her clit. Sobbing gasps of pleasure began to wrack her body. Her thighs shook, her virgin sheath clenching ever tighter around his thrusting finger.

She screamed Strax's name when she came, nearly yanking the hair from his scalp—but that was a blessing, because darkness was encroaching and the pain was a bright flare against it. After a final lick, Strax slowly moved upward, where she clasped his face and kissed him with wild heat and ravenous greed.

His wife still needed. And he was not done. Chest heaving with effort, he rasped against her mouth, "Shall I take you now, Mara, as a man takes his woman?"

"Yes," she all but sobbed, wrapping her legs around his hips. *"Now."*

His rigid cock pressed against her entrance and he thrust forward. But the weakness overtaking his muscles defeated his attempt. Her tightness didn't admit him, and his shaft rode over the wetness of her cunt to lay throbbing against her stomach.

Strax could do no more—nothing except roll to the side so she wouldn't be crushed beneath his massive bulk. With the last of his strength, he told her, "Ease your need upon me, my wife."

Because whether sleep took him or death did, Strax had no doubt his cock would remain as steel for her use.

He had but one last moment to look at Mara, to

witness her burning flame. To feel her soft lips against his, her gentle hand upon his cheek, and see the tears filling her eyes.

Then the darkness swept in.

SHE HAD NOT KILLED HIM. Strax discovered that truth when he awoke, though his parched tongue and the hunger grasping at his stomach told him that at least two days had passed. His furs covered him from head to toe, and when he tossed them aside, he discovered that she'd taken his horse, his supplies—even his boots and leathers.

All she had left behind were the furs, and that pleased him not at all. Even though Mara had taken his clothes and the horses' saddle blankets, each night she would have been cold. She ought to have left him exposed; Strax would have survived it, and preferred freezing to knowing she had been chilled.

He sat up and something tumbled from his chest to his bare lap. A gold coin. He only glanced at it a moment before examining his cock. The seed he'd spilled while feasting upon her cunt had dried on his shaft. If she'd used him, that seed wouldn't have remained. And there might have been virgin's blood instead. But there was none. So his wife was two days ahead of him, alone and unsatisfied, and shivering through the nights. A poor husband he'd proven to be.

A clever wife she'd proven to be.

Strax could not stop his laugh as he palmed the gold

coin and rose to his feet. No doubt she believed he'd be forced to return to Wintermere for another horse and supplies. His wife was clever, indeed.

But she didn't know everything. She didn't know that everyone who'd grown up in the Dead Lands scratched their living from wastelands even more barren than Lonewood.

So he rolled up his furs, because tying them around his waist would only slow him down. Instead he propped the bedroll onto his shoulder.

And wearing only a grin, Strax began to run.

MARA the FALLEN

The Skull Cliffs

For four days, Mara rode through Lonewood's wasteland. Within her was an emptiness that seemed as cursed and as lonely as the crooked tree that reigned over the realm, because her heart no longer filled her chest. Instead it had been torn apart, and one piece resided thousands of miles to the southwest, where her family was imprisoned in Solegius's dungeon. The bloody remainder of her heart was a few days' ride behind her, in the hands of a barbarian who should have been her enemy.

If Strax knew what she planned now, Mara had no doubt he'd do everything in his power to stop her. His blood oath demanded that he not allow the gauntlet to fall into the hands of anyone unworthy of wielding its power. So Mara had only herself to rely upon.

On either end of the Skull Cliffs, the northern oceans spilled over into the southern seas. Even Lonewood's cursed tree couldn't suck all the life from the mists of those waterfalls. A lush forest grew near the base of the Skull Cliffs, and seemed in the midst of summer instead of early spring. Riots of blooming wildflowers perfumed the warm air, their colors more brilliant than Mara had ever seen, and she only had to reach out to pluck ripened fruits from branches as she rode.

But although beauty met her gaze at every turn, horror awaited her. Nearly a dozen warriors lay dead at the bottom of the cliffs. She recognized some from the coliseum when the tournament had begun. Others were impossible to identify, because the fall from the cliffs had shattered their bones and pulped their flesh.

Mara couldn't afford to delay her quest, but neither could she leave the warriors to rot. So she spent a full day cutting wood for a large funeral pyre before darkness forced her to stop. In the morning she would finish, then begin her climb up the cliffs.

Lying in bed, she tried not to picture those mangled bodies. Tried not to picture herself falling, too. Yet picture it was all she did, and she lay shivering beneath her covers, her body bathed in the cold sweat of terror.

She didn't know when her shivers eased. It was full

dark and she was in a fitful sleep when warmth blanketed her restless form. She roused only a little as firm lips pressed to hers, as Strax's gruff voice rumbled in her ear. No arms held her tight, but she slept without fear knowing that he was near.

At dawn, she woke beneath heavy furs and to the sight of her husband wearing a saddle blanket tied around his waist and dragging the last of the corpses atop the pyre. Happy tears filled her eyes, and she blinked them away before Strax could see. She shouldn't be glad he was here.

Yet she was. And his dark gaze held no anger for her, though she'd drugged him with her cunt and stolen all his possessions. Instead the corners of his mouth tilted upward as he pulled Mara to her feet, but that smile didn't crack the grim stone of his expression.

He gestured a short distance away, where his gelding and her mare had joined a larger herd that grazed the lush meadow. "More than thirty horses."

Because more than thirty warriors had attempted the cliffs and left their mounts at its base. Apparently few warriors—if any—had returned from the keep and ridden away. "There is no ladder, either," said Mara. The ancient rope that should have hung down the face of the cliff was braided from the gods' hair, and was legendary for being as light as a feather and as strong as steel.

"The first warrior to reach the top likely pulled the ladder up with him so the others were forced to climb." His strong jaw hardened as he looked to the bodies atop the funeral pyre, and Mara did not need to ask what angered him. Any warrior who would draw up the ladder must have intended not only to slow the other contestants, but also to eliminate them.

The missing ladder told her something more, though. Because if a warrior retrieved the gauntlet from Khides' keep, he would return to the cliff and toss the ladder back down. That no ladder hung down the cliff face meant not a single warrior had succeeded. Most likely, they were all dead.

And Mara was next. A shiver of dread wracked her body, pulling Strax's warm gaze to her face. Softly he tipped her chin up and kissed her—but only a gentle, sweet kiss that lasted no longer than a breath. Because a dozen warriors lay lifelessly not far away, and this was neither the time nor the place for more.

Perhaps it would never be. Even if she survived the cliffs, after Strax discovered her intentions, he might never kiss her again.

The pain of that filled her heart. "I cannot linger here. It is three days' climb to the top," she said, and braced herself for what would come next.

Strax nodded. "You light the pyre. I'll prepare our supplies."

That was all he said, but Mara knew more would follow. Her heart aching, she waited for the rest.

Eyebrows pulling together in a frown, he brushed his thumb over her trembling lips. "What troubles you, wife?"

"You do, husband," she replied in a thick voice. "Because I would rather hear your doubts now than listen to them while I'm dangling from the cliff."

His frown darkened. "My doubts?"

"When you tell me I ought to give up. When you claim I will fall, or that I am not strong enough or clever enough to reach the top." Mara meant to spit each word at him, but to her horror, burning tears filled her eyes as she spoke. Desperately she turned her face away, but his strong hands cradled her cheeks and made her look up at him.

"Mara." Her name was a hoarse rasp, his eyes tormented as he searched her expression. "I *know* you are strong enough and clever enough. I have no doubt you can succeed."

"I cannot believe you." The tears spilled over her lashes. "You have told me so many times that I cannot win. From the first day we met, you doubted me—and told me so. And you never stopped telling me."

His eyes closed. As if in agony, a harsh groan ripped from his chest, and suddenly he pulled her close, his arms wrapping her tight. Mara wished she were strong enough to tear away from that embrace, but she could only bury her face against his shoulder and helplessly weep.

"No, Mara." Soothing fingers stroked down her back. "The first day, I doubted. And do you remember what you said to me?"

She did, clearly. Shuddering sobs wracked her reply.

"To leave me alone…and to go piss in your own eye."

"That, too." A laugh shook through him, then his voice deepened and his fingers threaded through her hair, tipping her tear-stained face back to meet his earnest gaze. "You told me that every doubt I uttered would only make you fight harder. And that every time I said that you would lose, you would only become more determined to win."

She *had* said those things. Lips parted, she stared up at him, suddenly afraid to hope what his words might mean. Afraid she might be wrong.

Strax must have read the uncertainty and fear upon her face. "Only a fool would doubt you, Mara. It is true that I did the first day, but every day since you've proved me wrong. I have watched you overcome every obstacle in your path these past six months—but even before the first week had passed, your strength and cleverness and determination won my heart." His thumbs stroked away the new tears that fell upon her cheeks, and his voice roughened. "Yet now I understand why speaking of my love hurt you. I *was* a fool, to see all that you are and yet not know that every time I meant to encourage you, instead I wounded you."

Encourage her? Mara couldn't stop the short, painful laugh that broke from her. Nor could she stop the hope that continued to grow within the lonely, empty wasteland where her heart had been.

"Then you…believe in me?" she whispered hesitantly. "You believe I might win?"

"I do." His gaze was unwavering. "In truth, when this contest began, I didn't believe anyone could defeat the guardians at Khides' keep and take the gauntlet. But I now believe that, of all the warriors who entered the tournament, you are the only one who *could* win. Because you do not seek riches or glory. Instead love has brought you here, Mara."

Love for her family. It *had* brought her here. But she still couldn't believe that made any difference. "That is not magic."

"It *is*, Mara," Strax said. "Magic is nothing but an invisible force that reshapes the world. Sorcerers use their spells—but love and hate reshape the world, too. You must have seen that is true."

She had. And yet it was not the same. "But a spell can make the impossible true."

"Since love is also magic, why can't it make the impossible true, too?" he asked in maddeningly reasonable tone. "Whether you believe or not, Mara, it is truth that a sorcerer's corrupted magic has no power within Khides' keep. But you wield the purest and most powerful kind of magic. And of all the warriors who have attempted to take the gauntlet, Khides is most likely to favor one such as you. The skulls behind us are her warning to anyone who would abuse their power—and you have come to save everyone you love from a tyrant."

Emotion constricted Mara's throat even as hope bloomed full and bright inside her chest. Strax genuinely sounded as if he believed in her. Yet after so many months, it was difficult to trust that he meant every word. No matter how she wanted to.

And she desperately wanted to. Because if Strax did… then he might genuinely love her, too.

Strax must have seen the war between hope and doubt that waged within her, because he demanded no answer. He only kissed her softly again before stepping back. "Light the pyre, Mara."

She did, releasing the warriors to the sky before returning to the base of the cliffs, where Strax rolled several days' worth of food into his furs.

Mara bent to unlace the boots she'd stolen from him, then stripped his leathers down her legs. His dark eyes burned with hunger when she glanced up again, though he made no move to touch her.

"The mornings are still cold, Mara, so keep wearing them," he said, but she shook her head.

"My bare feet are better for climbing." The boots were too thick and heavy. Already she could see how many small cracks and ledges her fingers and toes would have to find. "And no matter how tightly I tie them, your leggings tend to fall down and tangle around my knees. I cannot risk them doing so now."

His eyes darkened. "I will be directly below you. If you slip, I will catch you."

That declaration warmed her through, but he might soon regret such a promise. "It is three days' climb," she reminded him. "And I have no cock to point into the wind."

His shout of laughter echoed off the cliffs. "I would catch you even after you piss on me, wife. But if you give me warning, I will move to the side."

"I will," Mara said with a grin, then nearly choked on a wave of emotion when she realized this would be the first obstacle she and Strax would face together.

Except for the storm upon the sea, where he'd kept her from washing overboard. And the freezing nights in the mountains, where they'd kept each other warm. Those obstacles weren't part of the tournament…yet they had faced those together, too, and survived.

Now she helped him strap the bundle of furs and supplies to his back. After it was done, she tilted her head up and up and up, searching for the top of the cliffs, yet from the bottom they seemed to pierce the sky itself. Her stomach coiled into sick knots and clammy terror tightened her skin.

Strax caught her face and brought her gaze back down to his. "Shall I encourage you, Mara?"

Prod her along by telling her that she could not do this? Throat aching, she shook her head.

"Not in that way," he told her softly. "Never will I hurt you again with such careless words. Instead I will tell you that in these past days, I have thought of nothing but the sweetness of your cunt…and of how you begged for my cock."

Fire raced through her veins, burning away the

clammy fear. Because she had thought of his touch, too. Every night, trying to warm herself with the memory of his mouth and finding release with her fingers, yet still feeling so cold and alone.

His thumb swept across her lower lip, his eyes like smoldering embers. "When we reach the top, Mara—I will finally take you as a husband takes his wife."

That was fine encouragement, indeed. Heart pounding, she rose onto her toes for a kiss—the first she had sought from him. But she vowed it would not be the last.

He encouraged her again that night, when they found a narrow ledge to share. As Strax spread a healing poultice over her bleeding fingers and toes, he told her in how many places he would kiss her, and how many ways he would have her, and how many times he would make her come.

By the second night, even Strax's toughened hands needed tending. Winds buffeted the upper rim of the eye socket where they stopped and huddled together, wrapped in his furs. There Strax encouraged her again, describing their return to Aremond together, with her belly already heavy with his child. Telling her that they would discover a way to defeat Solegius and save her family, and together they would forge a life free of that king's tyranny.

Through it all, Mara held Strax close and dreamed with him—but fearing that she would lose her husband before she ever truly had him, could not admit she had already discovered a way to defeat Solegius.

On the third day, storm clouds thundered overhead

and rain lashed the face of the cliff. Each crack and ledge became treacherously slick. Soaked to her skin and trembling with exhaustion, Mara slowly crawled upward, terrified that if she looked down, Strax would no longer be there. He was each time, but she couldn't stop glancing down to be certain, though the endless distance to the bottom made her dizzy.

So often did Mara glance down that she almost never looked up, except to find the next handhold. When her fingers dug into wet dirt instead of ancient bone, she almost didn't understand what it meant. Then realization struck her all at once.

They'd nearly reached the top. Almost crying with relief, she carefully made her way upward to the cliff's edge. Here the climb was more treacherous than the rest, the soil from above muddy and crumbling. The sun had set, and the oncoming night made each handhold harder to see. Flashes of lightning threw confusing shadows, creating illusions of cracks and ledges where there were none. Forever it took Mara to climb the remaining distance, but at last she pulled herself up over the edge and onto her stomach.

Immediately she looked for the rope ladder and found it heaped into a giant pile a short distance away. Still on her belly, Mara turned to glance over the edge. Strax was only a few feet below.

She laughed down at him. "You are last again!"

He grinned and gripped a small bone ledge. "I am

exactly where I wish to be. Three days I have spent looking up at your sweet cunt, awaiting the moment I sheathe my cock deep."

Anticipation quivered over her skin. "Then wait there a moment longer, and I'll bring the ladder to you," she told him, her heart jumping when a thick river of mud spilled from the loosening soil below her head. "These last handholds are—"

Treacherous. With a scream, Mara lurched for Strax's hand as the small ledge he held disintegrated before her eyes. Her fingers locked around his wrist and she desperately pulled him back against the face of the cliff. His biceps bulged as he found a tiny ledge to grip with the fingers of his left hand. Mud slicked the rocks near his feet and she watched him attempt to find purchase, but every foothold crumbled the instant he put weight on it.

"Reach for the root," Mara cried out. A tree root coiled like a rope through the soil above his left hand, thick enough to hold him—and she didn't think the narrow ledge he gripped would support him much longer. Both of her hands were wrapped around his wrist but she was only steadying him; he bore his entire weight on three fingers, his massive body dangling thousands of feet above the ground.

Suddenly he went still, and when his gaze met hers, she choked out a denial of what she saw there before he spoke a word.

"Let go, wife."

She would die first. "Grab the root," she begged him.

His gaze was calm, his voice resolute. "If I do, you'll bear all of my weight and I'll pull you over the edge. Let go."

"Grab the root!" she snapped. "That ledge won't hold you much longer."

"And when it breaks, you'll fall with me. So let go."

"I'm strong enough to hold you."

"I know, Mara." His eyes seemed to be memorizing her face. Emotion thickened his voice. "You are so very strong. But I am heavy."

"Because your head is stuffed with rocks." A panicked, sobbing breath escaped her when he adjusted his grip— because the ledge was cracking beneath his fingers. "You said love was the most powerful magic. Do you truly believe that?"

"I do." His gaze locked on hers and agony ripped through her heart, because she knew he didn't intend to look away again, so her face would be the last thing he saw. "But loving you cannot stop a rock from breaking. It can only give me the strength to save you."

By sacrificing himself? She would never let him. "Then you must believe love can give me the strength to save *you.*" Desperately she gripped his wrist tighter. "Believe that I can do this, Strax. *Please.* Because if loving you means that I wield strong magics, then I must be the most powerful sorcerer in the world."

She must be. Because only minutes before, her arms had been shaking with fatigue and she'd barely had the strength to climb. Yet when heart-stopping emotion suddenly blazed in Strax's eyes and he let go of the crumbling ledge, his muscular bulk weighed nothing at all. For an endless moment she held him suspended, then his fingers gripped the root. With a mighty heave, Strax launched his upper body over the edge.

In the next instant she was in his arms. Strax surged to his feet, carrying her up with him and striding away from the cliff. Mara's body shook uncontrollably as she clung to his broad shoulders. With her legs wrapped tightly around his waist, she frantically kissed his cheeks and jaw and forehead and nose, sobbing and laughing at once.

So close she had come to losing him. So very close.

Remembered terror clawed at her heart. With sudden ferocity, Mara twisted her fingers in Strax's thick hair. Her warrior came to an abrupt halt, and she shoved her face close to his so he couldn't mistake her next words. "I will never let you go," she vowed through clenched teeth. *"Never."*

Savage pleasure burned in his dark eyes. His big hands squeezed her bare ass, grinding her against the steely length bulging beneath his leathers. "Then you'd best hold on tight, wife. Because I do not intend to stop until you have no strength left at all."

"I would like to see you try, warrior," Mara said in both truth and challenge, eager for her husband to fuck her until she was quivering and boneless, but also knowing he could never take all her strength, because it had never resided in her limbs.

Instead her strength lay in her heart, which was full to bursting with joy and love, and which raced at a head-spinning pace as his mouth claimed hers. Scorching need heightened with every possessive stroke of his tongue past her lips, and it seemed that the three days of peril against the cliff had only been preparation for this moment, clinging to Strax as if her very life depended upon it while his kiss pushed her higher and higher.

With a groan, Strax tore his mouth from hers. "You shiver with cold." His gaze searched through the sheets of falling rain as he pivoted, frustration hardening his features. "You need shelter from this storm."

A white flash of lightning illuminated their surroundings. Only bare earth stretched as far as could be seen, except for a few trees behind them, nearer to the cliff. Though their branches might provide protection from the rain, she knew he would not take her there, not so close to the edge.

But it was not the rain that made her shiver, anyway. Instead it had been the terror of nearly losing him. Now she only trembled with desire.

Mara caught his face and brought his gaze back to hers. "Your body covering mine is all the shelter I need."

Raw lust ignited the look Strax gave Mara then, and he set her on her feet. "I will cover you," he said in a voice harsh with need. "But I will not fuck you in the mud."

Mara wouldn't care if he did. But she stepped aside as

he tore loose the straps fastening the bedroll to his back. The contents of the bundle scattered when he roughly shook out the furs, readying their bed while Mara readied herself. Gripping the hem of her tunic, she pulled it over her head. Rain pelted her bare skin, yet the chill couldn't touch her when Strax glanced over and his heated gaze fell upon her nakedness. He went utterly still, except for his eyes that slowly looked their fill.

Boldly she stood before him with hot lust coursing through her blood and rain streaming from her hair. Even while following her across the Faren desert, Strax hadn't appeared as thirsty to her as he did now, as water sluiced over her shoulders and down the slopes of her breasts to drip from their hardened pink tips.

"Never have I seen beauty such as yours, Mara." His voice was hoarse, as if simply looking upon her an agonizing pleasure.

Just as the sight of Strax was such an acute pleasure to Mara. The storm raging overhead could never match the elemental power that her husband possessed. Like a mountain he was, so tall and strong, his fists like boulders. Lightning split the sky, revealing in stark contrast the steely ropes of muscles in his arms, the planes and ridges of his torso. Yet that electric flash was a dim candle next to the fire of his eyes when he stared at her.

Hunger replaced the thirst in his gaze when her fingers drifted down her belly, sifting through her rain-wet curls to find the part of her that was truly drenched.

"I am ready for you, husband," she told him huskily.

"If you are not, soon you will be." Tearing open the laces tying his leathers, he strode toward her. Through the dizzying anticipation of his approach, she glimpsed the ferocious rise of his cock, as massive and as primal as the barbarian who wielded it.

He was a fearsome size, yet Mara could never fear any part of this man she loved. Not his strength when he dragged her hand away from her cunt. Not his ravenous growl as he licked her arousal from her fingers. Not the possessive fire in his eyes when his own fingers delved between her thighs.

A groan tore from his chest. "A treasure of a wife you are, Mara. Not just hot and wet, but eager."

So eager. And Strax was already stealing her strength as he'd promised, for when he speared two thick fingers inside her, Mara trembled. When his thumb circled her clit, her knees buckled—yet he caught her before she fell, as she knew he always would.

With his left arm wrapped around her waist, Strax carried her to the furs, and with every step the fingers of his right hand stoked her hotter. Her cunt was a blazing furnace of heat and need as he laid her back and then followed her down, pushing her thighs wide.

Braced above her on one arm, Strax fisted his engorged length and lowered his hips between her parted thighs. A greedy moan erupted from her throat as he slicked the thick tip of his shaft through her folds, wetting himself with her arousal before fitting that broad head to her entrance.

Her fingernails digging into his biceps, Mara whimpered with anticipation. There her husband abruptly stilled, as if the sound she'd made was of pain. He made a soothing noise, but to Mara, Strax was the one who required soothing. His big body shook as he hovered over her, his every muscle corded from the effort of his restraint, his gaze frenzied with need even as he gently touched her face.

Through gritted teeth he said, "This will only hurt but once, wife."

She didn't care if it hurt a thousand times. Mara would always lift her body toward his as she did now, preparing to sheathe his turgid length. Yet he still hesitated, his broad crown demanding entry but not accepting her invitation.

With a short laugh, she arched toward him again. "You have overcome so many obstacles on this journey, husband—dangerous seas and freezing mountains and treacherous cliffs. Will you let a maidenhead defeat you now?"

His jaw tightened, his face a harsh mask of hunger. She gasped as his hips flexed and he pressed forward—yet too gently.

Immediately he eased back, a groan wracking his rigid form. "Your cunt is tighter than a fist."

So it was. "And if you do not push harder than that, your fist is all you will ever fuck."

A laugh shook his big body against hers. "Do not tease me, wife. I cannot bear to hurt you, and I have little control left."

"Then you have too much." Raising her head, she gently bit his bottom lip before sliding her tongue across his teeth. Her fingers raked down his straining back, her thighs squeezing his hips. "A little pain I can bear. What I cannot bear is how you hold yourself back from me now. Not after I almost lost you."

As if remembering, a shudder tore through his massive body. His fierce gaze locked on hers. "Say it again."

No question what he meant. "I love you, Strax," she told him softly. "So take me as a warrior takes a woman as strong as I am."

The sky flashed white, separating his features into stark shadows and laying bare his tormented need as, with one savage thrust, he buried his cock deep. Mara's scream was lost in the crack of thunder. Taking Strax was no easier than any of this journey had been. But this time she didn't have to bear her pain alone and in misery. Instead it was accompanied by sheer joy—and by pleasure, the greatest she'd ever known, because Strax was in her arms, and so the pain of his possession was nothing at all.

"Mara?" His rigid frame shook with the strain of remaining motionless as her inner muscles struggled to adjust to his thick girth.

"I am here," she reassured him, panting, then kissed him fiercely as he withdrew and shoved deep again, spearing her with pleasure. Crying out, she arched her hips, loving the burning stretch each time her body yielded to his. *"More."*

As if her ragged plea stole the last of his control, he claimed her mouth in a devastating kiss and relentlessly stroked his swollen length into her welcoming heat. Lightning flashed again, but this time it came from within her, a storm of ecstasy that was twisting higher and higher.

Strax seized her ass in his brutish grip when she began to writhe. Ruthlessly he held her in place for every powerful thrust, and the pace he set was like the pounding of a war drum. Had he still been her enemy, this brutal rhythm might have demanded her surrender, her submission. But an answering beat thrummed through Mara's veins, hot and thick. Because no war remained between them, and this night he had almost lost her, but a warrior will never be separated from his wife—so the untamed ferocity of their mating was not a fight, but a declaration that nothing could rend them asunder. The pounding of his cock, her hands clawing his shoulders, the ravenous hunger of their kiss were a battle cry announcing that they were one, and a warning to anything that might try to stand against them.

Lightning sizzled through her again as Strax wedged his hand between their bodies, his teeth gritted and his eyes feral. Mara cried out as his rough fingers stroked her clit, arching beneath him in electric pleasure. When his hips jolted forward and buried his cock to the hilt, the orgasm rolled though her like thunder, drenching his length in a carnal rush. Head thrown back, Strax groaned and thrust into her clenching sheath once, twice before roaring his climax into the storm above, his shaft pulsating within her. So hot. So deep.

Almost endlessly it seemed, Strax filled her with his seed. Each scorching pulse renewed the shudders of ecstasy tearing through Mara's senses, until she lay boneless and quivering in his arms.

He kissed her then, hot and slow, his strong hands cupping her face. And when her warrior lifted his head, his gaze locked on hers, she knew the truth of his every word even before he said, "I love you, Mara."

Every time before, that declaration had hurt. This time Mara only knew joy, because she believed. So she kissed him, and held him close, and knew for certain that not only did he love her—but that love would make the impossible true.

And that it was magic, too.

STRAX the BELIEVER

The Skull Cliffs

WHILE THE STORM RAGED ABOVE, THREE TIMES DID Strax take his wife. Her pleasured cries still rang in his ears and her sweet cunt still clutched his cock when the rain abruptly stopped and he no longer needed to serve as her shelter, but her bed. He rolled onto his back and loved the feel of her slight weight atop his chest, her head pillowed on his shoulder.

His cock stirred within her sultry heat, but he wouldn't fuck her again. Not until morning. His Mara was strong, but for three days she had exhausted herself against the face of the cliff—and the most dangerous task was yet to come.

He expected her to sleep now, yet the absent play of her fingers in his hair told him that her mind was too occupied for slumber. So with a soft grunt, he told her, "Speak to me, Mara."

One day, she might without prompting. But for so long on this journey she'd been alone—it was his own fault that she was unaccustomed to relying on anyone but herself.

Now she lifted her head to look down at him. Beneath the nighttime sky, her beautiful face was but a play of shadows and darkness, yet he could still see the soft gleam of her teeth as she hesitantly bit her bottom lip before saying, "I won't give the gauntlet to Solegius."

Relief slipped through his heart, because Strax knew not what he'd have done if she'd insisted upon giving that weapon to the tyrant. Yet his heart ached, too, because he knew what the cost of her decision might be.

Still he tried to reassure her. "We *will* free your family," he vowed. "We will discover a way."

"I have," she said softly, her fingers tracing his jaw. "I intend to wear the gauntlet and destroy him."

Tension locked his muscles. "You intend to wear it?"

Biting her lip again, she nodded. "After you told me of your clan's blood oath to prevent anyone who would misuse the gauntlet's power from wielding it, I thought… you did not believe in me, so you would never trust me with that power. I drugged you so that you wouldn't be forced to stop me."

The sweetest poisoning he'd ever known. "So that you could race ahead to Khides' keep."

"Yes," she whispered now. "I must free my family, and you must prevent anyone unworthy from wielding the gauntlet. I thought it would be impossible for us to both have what we needed. But you love me and believe in me, so perhaps the impossible can be true. If I were to win the gauntlet, I could take it back to Aremond and destroy Solegius and his warlords. And you could remain with me, and make certain that I never misuse its power."

That was truth. And it wasn't the thought of Mara wielding the gauntlet that made Strax pause, but what might happen if it ever fell into another's hands. A powerful queen was the first woman Khides had given the gauntlet to, and she'd used it fairly and wisely. Then the queen had given it to her twin sons, who'd broken the world.

So that must be Strax's duty now—to see that the gauntlet never left Mara's possession.

He had been quiet too long. Painful doubt shadowed her gaze, and she averted her face.

"Perhaps it will not matter," she said in a raw voice. "I might die trying to retrieve the gauntlet from Khides' keep."

Strax caught her chin, made her look at him again as he vowed, "Then I will die helping you, wife."

MARA

the

CHAMPION

In the morning, Mara was awakened by Strax in the manner a husband should wake his wife, then he sheathed his cock deep while she was still shuddering from the pleasure of his tongue. Her lips were swollen and hot from his kisses, her nipples sensitive to the barest touch, and the muscles of her inner thighs ached in the same way they had during the first week of the tournament, before she'd become accustomed to riding all day.

For the first time since the tournament had begun, Mara allowed herself to linger in bed. But her duty could not be denied, nor the danger that lay ahead.

Mara's heart filled with both anticipation and dread when they began to walk toward Khides' keep. Strax had vowed to help her retrieve the gauntlet. Now she quelled the impulse to drug him again so that he could not risk himself, knowing that nothing she said or did would stop her husband from entering the keep at her side.

The sun was high overhead when the structure appeared in the distance, yet it was nothing as she had expected. Time had worn away the tower's thick walls, leaving only ring of stone rubble…and a mountainous pile of skulls in front of the entrance.

Fear trembled through Mara at the sight, yet her steps didn't waver as she and Strax continued their approach. He had told her that, through the ages, thousands of warriors had tried and failed to retrieve the gauntlet from the keep. Now their skulls served as a warning to anyone foolish enough to attempt the same.

With trepidation shaking through her veins, she asked Strax, "Have you been here before?"

Expression grim, he shook his head and took her hand. "I'll try for the gauntlet first."

"No," she said softly, squeezing his fingers. "We'll try together. And we *will* succeed."

Strax nodded, but his face was a mask of indecision and torment as they reached the pile of skulls. At the bottom lay a fine dust of ancient crumbling bone, the skulls bleached white. Nearer the top were skulls with dried flesh and hair still clinging—and the bloodied heads of warriors who'd entered the tournament.

Yet one contestant still lived. Mara's mouth dropped open as she reached the top of the skulls and looked down at the bottom of the pile, where a warrior paced outside the ring of stone rubble that marked the ancient walls of the keep. Within the circular keep was only bare earth, perhaps thirty paces across. At its center was an obsidian altar, upon which the gauntlet lay.

Standing near the ruins on either side of the ring were two stone statues—the guardians Strax had mentioned. Unlike the keep walls, the marble warriors showed no signs of decay. Twice the height of any man, the guardians each wore sculpted armor and a helmet carved to resemble a wolf's head.

The wolf brothers of legend, Mara realized. The twins who'd broken the world while fighting over the gauntlet. Strax had said they were kings, not wolves…yet she saw why legend knew them as both. Now the stone brothers watched over the gauntlet—as punishment or penance, Mara couldn't guess.

She took a step and a skull tumbled down the pile, alerting the warrior below. He whirled around. Surprise filled his expression, and he drew his sword as if warding her away.

"Stop there!"

She did, but only waiting for Strax to catch up. Faintly she recognized the warrior. Ferinit, she thought his name was.

Below, the warrior shook his head in disbelief. "*You* made it so far? I believed you dead—and thought I was the last!"

"No," Mara replied with a laugh. "Strax is always last."

Her husband appeared over the top of the mountain of skulls as she said so. Ferinit's gaze flicked to the barbarian and the surprise on the warrior's face became dismay. Likely because the sword he pointed at her seemed not so threatening now, not with a man like Strax at her side.

Mara carefully began to make her way down the shifting pile of skulls. "You have not attempted to reach the gauntlet?"

"No. I was hoping to discover a way…I have seen the others—I have seen…" Ferinit trailed off as a haunted expression emptied his face. Then his jaw hardened with determination and he glanced toward the altar. "You won't steal the prize from me!"

The tournament prize? "Trust me, warrior, it is not gold that I seek—"

Mara broke off, her breath catching when Ferinit suddenly leapt over the ruined wall and into the keep's inner circle. Heart thundering, she looked at the marble guardians. Neither statue moved.

Whether Mara and Strax pursued him seemed to concern Ferinit more than the guardians did. He raced toward the altar, throwing glances over his shoulder to where she and Strax were descending the mountain of skulls.

Strax caught Mara's hand, steadying her through the final layer of ancient bone that crushed to dust beneath her feet. His gaze, too, was on the stone guardians. "He saw what happened to the others, yet doesn't fear the statues?"

Apparently not. Yet even as Mara opened her mouth to respond, Ferinit reached the altar and his behavior changed. Where he'd been rushing, now he hesitated—looking to each of the guardians before glancing wildly back at Strax and Mara.

"The guardians must delay their attack until after the gauntlet is taken," she realized. And whatever form that attack took, Ferinit was visibly preparing himself to grab the gauntlet and run—and he was also visibly terrified, tearing his fingers through his dark hair, then reaching for the gauntlet before snatching his hands back.

Her own hands clammy with dread, Mara called out, "Tell us how, warrior, and we will help you!"

Ferinit made no response, except to square his shoulders—as if the sound of Mara's voice only hurried him to claim the prize before they could. He swept the gauntlet up against his chest and turned to run.

"Mara," Strax's deep voice was urgent with warning. The statues at either side of the bare circle of earth began to move. Yet slowly, so slowly. Surely too slowly to reach Ferinit before he cleared the keep's wall.

Mara's gaze flicked back to the warrior and horror gripped her throat. Ferinit should have been halfway across the clearing by now, but he'd only made it a single pace away from the altar. Now he seemed to be crawling across the dirt, the gauntlet clutched to his chest, desperation reddening his face. But he wasn't crawling—instead he struggled against the multitude of hands and arms that had erupted out of the ground and were pulling him down into the parting earth, as if dragging him into a grave. Some hands were nothing but skeletal bones, some rotting, some newly dead. As if the skulls of everyone who'd tried to claim the gauntlet were piled in a mountain…and the remainder of their bodies now guarded the weapon they'd tried to take.

Frantically she looked to Strax. The barbarian stood atop the ring of rubble. Before she could scream at him to stop, he leapt down into the keep's circle.

Nothing erupted from the ground to grab him. Casting her a triumphant glance, Strax drew his sword and raced toward Ferinit. Mara scrambled after him. The stone guardians steadily approached, each footstep a heavy thud that amplified the pounding within her chest. Ahead, Strax struck his blade through the macabre forest of arms pulling at Ferinit's legs.

As if he'd cut through shadows, Strax's sword harmlessly swept through the grasping arms. Futilely he tried again, then fell to his knees and attempted to grip one of the rotting hands wrapped around Ferinit's calf. Strax's fingers passed through the gory flesh as if it were nothing more than an illusion.

An illusion that Ferinit couldn't break away from.

They'd dragged him waist-deep into the earth. The warrior grunted with the strain of trying to break their grip, clawing at the dirt in front of him.

As one, Mara and Strax took hold of Ferenit—Strax wrapping an arm around his chest and Mara grabbing his wrist—and tried to haul him away from the grasping hands.

The moment they touched him, more arms erupted out of the ground to capture their ankles in bony shackles. The soil sank beneath Mara's feet. With a scream, she desperately hauled on Ferinit's wrist again—then Strax's big body tackled hers. They rolled away from the warrior, whose own hoarse scream of despair rang in her ears.

"If we are touching the gauntlet," Strax said on heaving breaths, "or touching someone who is, the keep will stop us."

Frantically Mara looked to the stone guardians. The wolf brothers were but a few paces away, their marble swords drawn. "We have to help him."

Strax nodded, his face a hard mask of determination as he stood and faced one of the statues. Like a bull he charged the massive legs, not attempting to strike the stone guardian with a blade but simply to slow it down or push it over—yet Mara was not surprised when even a man of Strax's might seemed no more to the guardian than a buzzing fly. It did not even swat him away but simply continued toward Ferinit as if the massive barbarian was not grunting and shoving against his marble waist, Strax's thick muscles bulging with effort.

Yet muscle was not the only strength a person could have, Mara knew. And her husband believed that only pure magics had any effect within the keep.

She couldn't claim to love Ferinit, but love wasn't the only strong magic she could wield. Kindness was, too.

Crouching before the struggling warrior, she urged him, "Let go of the gauntlet. You'll be free and we will try again together."

Another hoarse scream emerged from between Ferinit's gritted teeth as the hands dragged him farther down, so only his shoulders remained above the ground, the gauntlet wedged protectively under his neck.

Still he shook his head. "I can't let it go. You'll take it and leave me to die."

"No," she swore. "I vow that we will not."

Booted feet digging furrows out of the earth as he was pushed inexorably forward by the stone guardian, Strax barked a harsh warning. "Mara! Step back from him!"

Because the statues were almost upon them. Mara didn't move but steadily held Ferinit's frantic gaze. "Trust that I will not betray you. I have no need for the gold; instead my family is imprisoned in Solegius's dungeon and I intend to free them. I don't know why you entered the tournament—for riches or glory…or perhaps Solegius has threatened someone you love, too—but whatever it is you seek, we will make certain that you get it. But you must let us help you first. I swear we will not betray your trust."

Everything seemed to still. Focused on Ferinit, Mara

didn't realize the hands no longer dragged him down until she heard Strax's disbelieving "They've halted!" Their deadly fingers simply held Ferinit now—and on either side of him, the statues had frozen in place.

Had kindness done that? Truly?

On a shaky laugh, Mara held out her hand for Ferinit to take, so she could pull him to his feet. "See? We'll help you."

"No." The warrior shook his head. "You'll steal—"

Ferinit's scream cut off the rest. Mara shouted a denial as the hands dragged him deeper. Strax's steely arm snagged around her waist and pulled her back, kicking and fighting but knowing there was no help for the warrior now. Neck deep, only his head and his arms were above the ground, his hands still holding onto the gauntlet—until a stone guardian plucked the gauntlet out of his grip. The other sliced his sword through Ferinit's neck, sending his head flying.

The warrior's body disappeared into his grave. Her breath coming in ragged gasps, Mara stared at the spot where Ferinit had been…and didn't look back at the skull mountain to search for his head. Strax's powerful arms held her tight. His fingers shook as he turned her around, cupped her face in his big hands, searching her eyes as if to reassure himself that she was still there, still alive.

Movement drew their gazes to the stone guardian carrying the gauntlet. He placed it atop the altar, then he and his brother began their slow trek back to the edge of the keep's circle.

On a shaky breath, Mara whispered, "They stopped for a moment."

"Yes." Strax's answer was gruff. "For a moment."

"We should try now, since we are already in the keep." And while she still had the courage.

Tension whitened Strax's mouth. "Let me do it alone, Mara. If love is magic enough to stop them, then I have enough love for you to see me through this."

"I believe that, but I won't let you do it alone," she said firmly. "We'll try together."

Jaw tight, Strax pressed his forehead to hers. Torment roughened his voice. "Then I will carry you. When you take the gauntlet from the altar, the hands will drag me down. But I'll be strong enough to break free of them, Mara, and carry you to the edge of the keep. Just as you were strong enough to hold me at the cliff."

Mara hated that plan. But she knew her stubborn husband would accept no other. "If you cannot break free, I'll toss the gauntlet away and we'll try again another day."

Strax nodded, then kissed her fiercely, *so* fiercely, before sweeping her up into his arms. Cradling her against his chest, he strode toward the altar.

When he'd told her the gauntlet was forged from the hearts of gods, Mara had imagined a finely wrought piece of armor made of precious metals and stones. But the weapon on the obsidian block instead resembled a large leather glove, better suited to a blacksmith than a warrior.

Yet it held enough power to break the world…or to stop a tyrant sorcerer.

Mara couldn't take her eyes from the gauntlet as Strax halted in front of the altar. Her pulse raced at a sickly fast pace, and her husband cradled her so closely that she could feel the hammering of his heart through his thickly muscled chest. "Should I try to wear it right away?"

"It matters not if you do." His response was hoarse, as if forced through an obstruction in his throat. "Its power cannot be used within the keep."

Only pure magic could be wielded. Magic such as love and kindness.

Mara prayed theirs would be enough. With Strax's arms holding her tight, she reached out and claimed the gauntlet.

Instantly the world shifted——or the earth beneath her husband's feet did. Mara cried out as Strax began to stride forward, his teeth clenched with effort. One step. Two. Each one a mighty battle against the iron grip of the ghostly hands trying to drag him down. Three. Already he'd made more progress than Ferinit had, yet each step such a struggle that his pace was no faster than the stone guardians' in their direction, all of them locked in a slow race.

Her terrified gaze on the statues, Mara frantically chanted, "I love you, I love you," trying to give Strax any strength he needed, then shouted at the guardians, "I only want to free my family! I only want to free all of

Aremond from Solegius's rule, to help them!"

Just as she'd tried to help Ferinit. Yet this time, the statues did not halt, and the horrifying pull of the hands below never ceased.

And Strax was slowing. Teeth gritted, sweat streaming over his skin, he continued striding forward—but he was not carrying her so high above the ground now, Mara realized with horror. The hands had not stopped his forward movement but they'd been dragging him deeper, deeper, and the soil was up to his knees, forcing him not only to fight their grip but also to plow through the earth ahead. Now the stone guardians were closer to Strax and Mara than Strax and Mara were to the edge of the keep—and this was a race they could not win.

"I'll let the gauntlet go," Mara whispered brokenly and Strax nodded, his chest heaving, still straining too much to speak. "Tomorrow we'll try again."

However long it took. Throat tight, she hurled the gauntlet at the nearest statue—and the leather didn't leave her grip. *No.* She tried again. It stuck to her hand as if soldered. Wildly she tried to shake it off and then raised terrified eyes to Strax's face. "Ferinit said he couldn't let it go. I thought he meant he *wouldn't*, because he didn't trust us to help him. But he couldn't!"

Desperate fire lit Strax's gaze. Grunting, he surged forward, yet he was almost buried to his waist now, fighting for every inch.

No no no no. With sobbing breaths, Mara ripped at her

hand, trying to tear away the gauntlet—but although she could adjust her grip on the leather, she couldn't release it. The stone guardians were almost upon them, huge, unstoppable.

"Drop me," Mara begged Strax. "Leave me here and save yourself."

"As you did…upon the cliff?" Each word was a grunt from between clenched teeth and a grimace of effort that transformed his expression into a mad grin. *"Never."*

"Then know I love you," she whispered fiercely, clinging to him. "I love you…but love isn't enough."

That realization slammed into Mara even as the nearest guardian raised his sword, lupine helmet gleaming beneath the sun.

"It *is* enough, Mara," Strax denied, his arms holding her tighter, tucking her closer to his chest as if his heart could guard her from the blade about to descend upon her head. "I *will* carry you the distance."

And she believed he could. Never had Mara known anything as mighty as her husband's heart. But love was not all they needed now.

"Trust me, Strax," she implored softly, lifting her hand to his clenched jaw. "Trust me."

Abruptly he stopped…as did the guardians. The statues stood frozen with arms reaching for the gauntlet and swords swinging for their necks—and their blades halted only inches from Strax and Mara's heads. But the guardians didn't retreat. Instead they remained, as if waiting.

A sob of relief tore from Mara's throat. "Have the hands stopped pulling?"

Strax confirmed her hope with a short nod, amazement flaring through his expression. "They only hold me in place. What did you do?"

"I remembered the story you told me of the wolf brothers." Shaking in his arms, she tried not to look at how close the guardian's sword was to the back of Strax's neck, tried not to remember how quickly Ferinit had been killed and pulled under. "It wasn't kindness that stopped them before. I asked Ferinit to trust me. And that is the magic needed here. Because the brothers loved each other, but they didn't trust each other to wield the gauntlet's power wisely and fairly. And love is always weakened without trust."

"Yes," Strax agreed, but his gaze was on the guardian behind her. Carefully he turned her in his arms, shifting her weight to the opposite side. Putting himself in the path of the guardian's sword, Mara realized—so if the statue continued to swing, the blade would hit Strax instead of her.

She caught his face, made him meet her eyes. With her heart in her throat, she whispered thickly, "Do you *truly* trust me to wield this gauntlet?"

"I do," Strax replied, and the same fire that lit his gaze as he'd spoken his wedding vows burned brightly behind his eyes again. "I have watched you for months, Mara. I know the woman you are. And I trust that you will only use the weapon for reasons that are good and right."

Joy swept through Mara, because her husband so clearly believed every word he spoke—so clearly believed in her. But dread followed when the guardians still didn't retreat.

Heart thundering, she frantically looked between the statues. "You trust me to wield the gauntlet. Why isn't that enough?"

"Because the brothers needed to trust each other. Not just one trusting the other, but both." Strax's gruff reply swung her gaze back to his face, where bleak agony darkened his expression. "Forgive me, Mara. Forgive me."

Fear clutched her chest. "Forgive what? I trust you with the gauntlet."

She didn't believe Strax would ever wear it, unless he had no other choice—but even then, he'd never misuse its power. She believed that with all of her heart.

"Forgive me for not being a man you could believe in or trust." His voice roughened, his self-torment bare upon his face. "These past months, I have betrayed my heart again and again, rarely helping you though I could have eased your journey, hurting you with the words I spoke. Only a week past, you didn't even trust me to remove the enchanted collar without abusing my power over you, but held a knife to my throat until it was done. A few days of marriage cannot make up for six months, but I swear to you, Mara—you can trust that I will never betray my heart or you again."

Breath catching, Mara stared at him. Because he spoke

truth. A week past, she hadn't trusted him. Not his words, not his actions.

Yet since that day, her feelings had utterly changed. Before their marriage, she'd wished that Strax was a man who would comfort and help her, who would love her and believe in her.

Now she no longer wished, because Strax had proved over and over again he *was* that man.

"I do," she said boldly, gazing into his eyes—and realized this was what the guardians waited for. Because wearing the gauntlet wouldn't be the only way to wield it. "You have more power over me now than an enchanted collar could ever give, Strax, because I love you. But I trust that you will never abuse that power over me and make me misuse the gauntlet."

Strax's eyes closed. Mara's heart stopped. Then she saw his naked relief, and realized the hands had released him. The statues began to withdraw, and in the next moment she was laughing and crying as Strax carried her out of the keep. Once beyond the ruined wall, she threw the gauntlet onto the ground. His lust rose fiercely between them, and Mara kissed him with all the love bursting within her heart even as her body slickened with need.

Gently Strax lowered her to the sun-warmed grass, but there was no gentleness in his kiss or his hands as he shoved her tunic to her waist and ripped open his leathers.

"Say it," he demanded, releasing his massive length.

"I love you, Strax." She fisted her hands in his hair and

dragged his mouth back to hers. "I love you."

With a powerful thrust, he drove deep. Mara welcomed him with a glad cry against his mouth, her inner muscles clutching his thick cock as Strax fucked her in a frenzy of love and relief that soon turned to pure pleasure. She came, writhing and screaming beneath him, and he groaned her name as his pulsating length pumped her full of his seed.

His kiss gentled then, and he rolled until she lay atop him, grinning up at her. "You are a champion now, my wife."

Mara laughed, for indeed she had won the tournament. "I could not have done it without your help," she said truthfully, still in awe of the strength that had allowed him to carry her so far across the keep, and of his belief and trust that had allowed her this victory. Because she could never have claimed the gauntlet alone. Love only needed one, but trust took two.

Yet her journey was not over—and they could not linger here. Her family was still imprisoned in Solegius's dungeon and even if they traveled at a faster pace than they'd come, it was still a long distance back to Aremond.

On a sigh, she rose to her feet and picked up the gauntlet from where she'd thrown it down. So far she'd come for this. And there was still so far to go.

She felt Strax's gaze upon her as, her heart pounding, she slipped the weapon onto her hand. Though the leather made from the gods' hearts appeared stiff, the fit of the glove was supple around her fingers…and she felt no different. "It is many months' journey back to Aremond," she said. "I must learn to wield this in that time. But I don't even know where to begin."

"The gauntlet uses the magic of its wearer. So learn to focus yours," Strax suggested. "Think of your love for your family, your desire to free them."

So much love. For her brothers and sisters, her mother and father. Closing her eyes, she pictured their faces, and pure emotion surged through her chest.

She opened her eyes within a dark, dank cell. In front of Mara, her mother sat on the floor with her youngest siblings, scratching figures into the dirt. Teaching them to calculate sums. Her mother's dark hair was shorn close to her scalp, and Mara had a clear vision of her mother picking lice from tangled and greasy clumps, and felt her mother's despair and frustration and determination as she sliced through the long strands....and heard her father's warm voice telling her mother that she was as beautiful as ever to him.

I cannot give up now. I cannot give up now. I cannot give up now.

That was also her father's voice, not a memory but happening now—though not spoken aloud. Instead her father only thought it. Mara turned toward the sound and pain ripped through her heart when she saw his emaciated form. His eyes were on the door as he carefully, secretly sharpened a bit of stone, his mind filled with thoughts of using the blade to kill the cruel guards and to free his family, and at the same time Mara knew his fevered imaginings she also saw every bite that he'd given to his children, how many times he'd insisted he wasn't hungry even while his stomach seemed to gnaw holes in him from within.

"Mara?"

That was her eldest brother's voice, who looked at her now in confusion and uncertainty. But a pained cry pulled Mara's gaze to where her mother was staring at her, a trembling hand over her mouth and tears filling her eyes, her mind screaming denials and her heart already grieving—as if she believed Mara's appearance in this cell must mean her daughter was dead.

Then Mara's second sister whispered, "Are you a ghost?" and Mara shook her head.

Turning, she waved her gauntleted hand and the dungeon door exploded outward. With a flicker of her eyelashes, she slaughtered the guards who came running.

Mara wasn't a ghost. She was a champion…with the power of a god.

She went in search of Solegius.

STRAX
the
GUARDIAN

Khides' Keep

MARA LEFT HIM, YET SHE ALSO REMAINED. FOR THREE hours she hovered upright, her feet dangling above the ground. She was motionless except for her hair, which blew around her as if she were caught in a storm. Yet if there was a storm, Mara was the sun at the center, for her eyes and skin glowed brightly gold.

When she came back to him, it was sudden. The glow dimmed and Strax caught her as she fell out of the air. When she sank to her knees, he sank with her.

"It is done," she said in a thick voice, pulling the gauntlet from her hand. "Solegius and his warlords, his slavers…I killed them all."

Strax could hardly comprehend it. "All?"

She nodded, her chin wobbling. "I looked into their hearts and their minds, and if I saw nothing but cruelty, then I…" Her haunted gaze rose to meet his. "You trusted that I would always use the gauntlet for right and good. I think what I did was right. I don't know if it was good."

"That you wonder only makes me more certain of you," Strax said, his heart aching for her. Strax had fought in wars before, had seen many battles. He knew what nightmares tore at her now and would have done anything to spare her from them. But his Mara had not asked to be spared.

"I need to put it back," she whispered.

He frowned. "The gauntlet?"

She nodded. "I finished what I needed to do. And it terrifies me to know this much power is in one person's hands. Even if that person is me."

That she thought so was another reason Strax would never be afraid of that gauntlet in her possession. "Solegius will not be the only tyrant or sorcerer to ever threaten Aremond."

"No. But we will try to defeat any others through usual means." Wryly she smiled at him. "And if we cannot, we know where to find the gauntlet."

That was truth. So Strax kissed her, then walked with her back to the keep, stunned by the realization that his wife had held the gods' hearts in her hands and was willing to let them go. Yet she'd never let go of *his* heart, even to save herself.

Never had he loved her so much. Never had he felt so humbled by her love.

They faced no danger within the keep. When she placed the gauntlet onto the altar, the marble guardians knelt and bowed their heads in her direction. Mara blushed and appeared uncertain, but Strax thought they didn't show enough respect. The stone kings ought to have been crawling at her feet.

Outside the keep again, it seemed that a burden dropped from her shoulders. Never had he seen her smile so bright, her laugh so sunny. She told him how she had flown as a bird, and how after killing Solegius and his warlords, she had returned to her family's side to restore her father's strength and tell them she would be bringing a husband home with her. And all the while she spoke, such happiness shined from her, as if she still glowed… because she did.

Mara saw his fierce gaze upon her and slowly stopped, biting her lip. "I have just realized—before I gave up the gauntlet, I should have looked for your brother. To see… where he was."

Which she clearly believed was at the bottom of the Illwind Sea. Yet Strax knew Aruk had survived. He shrugged. "We will find one another again."

"You are so certain?"

Strax nodded, then caught her hand and drew it to his side, where the runes softly glowed with the power locked inside him. "These runes contain my magic beneath my skin, but I still can sense enchantments—just as I can always sense my twin, no matter how far he is. So I do not know where Aruk is, but I know that he lives."

"Oh." A laughing smile curved her soft mouth. "All this time, I thought you were too mule-brained to admit that he'd drowned."

Strax grinned. "I am that, too."

"Perhaps we'll find him on our journey back, then. He's bound by the same blood oath as you, so he might have continued following the tournament route…he might have…"

She fell silent, staring ahead, and Strax was not wholly surprised when her eyes filled with a golden light and power softly glowed from her skin.

Yet this time she did not leave him or hover above the ground. Instead she whispered, "I see him. He is… with a woman."

Strax snorted out a laugh. Yes, that was very much like Aruk.

A frown creased Mara's brow. "A red ribbon is wrapped around their hands. They're being married."

Strax's eyebrows shot upward. That was very much *not* like Aruk.

"He's in chains," Mara said, her voice full of sudden worry. "It appears he is being forced to marry."

At that, Strax shook his head. "Aruk has never been forced to do anything he did not wish to."

The glow faded from Mara's skin and she looked to him, blinking and confused. "I wasn't wearing the gauntlet," she said shakily.

She wasn't. But no one could wield so much power without it touching her in return. And perhaps she was not the only one the power had touched. Before she'd worn the gauntlet, Strax had spent his seed within her many times.

He drew her close, spreading his hand protectively over her belly. He'd sworn a blood oath to prevent anyone from misusing the gauntlet's power—the same power she *still* carried within her. Perhaps that power wasn't as strong as while wearing the glove, but it mattered little to him.

"Then you are well and truly caught, my wife," he said against her lips. "Even if you wish to rid yourself of me, always will I be your guardian. Protecting you will forever be my duty."

"I am your duty?" Eyes narrowed, she pushed playfully at his chest. "Then I say that you are my prize for winning this tournament."

Strax would never argue with that, though it was he who'd won the greatest treasure on this journey. And he suspected the journey ahead would be much slower and longer, with many mornings when they lingered in bed.

But there was no lingering now. Only urgent need as Mara pushed him down onto the grass, straddling him with the intention of claiming her prize.

Then claim him she did, embracing his swollen

length in a heaven of wondrous heat. Groaning, Strax thrust upward. Never had any man been so blessed as he was, to have such a wife, with a mind so clever and a cunt so tight. His heart pounded in his chest as his cock pounded inside her. Blunt fingers sifting through her curls, he stroked her clit to the same carnal rhythm, his enraptured gaze locked upon the exquisite beauty of her face. Like a summer storm his wife moved over him, hot and wet and fast.

When her eyes closed and her spine arched, her rose-tipped breasts lifting toward the sun, his love for her struck him so powerfully that only through sheer will did Strax halt the spurt of his seed. His treasure of a wife glowed fiercely with the strength of her pleasure, her convulsing sheath tightly clutching his shaft. Lost to the ecstasy of that passionate grip, he held back his release until her shudders passed.

Then Strax ended this journey exactly as he'd begun—believing that Mara was the most beautiful woman he'd ever beheld.

And by coming last.

MARA

the

QUEEN

Epilogue

MORE THAN A FULL YEAR PASSED BEFORE MARA AND Strax rode into the city at the heart of Aremond. The journey home had taken even longer than Mara had anticipated, and not only because she and Strax lingered in bed almost every morning. She ached to embrace each member of her family again, and to introduce them to her husband, but the desperate urgency that had driven her from the kingdom had been replaced by utter contentment.

Riding beside her, Strax cradled their daughter against his broad chest. The baby slept peacefully in a small bundle of furs, and every time Mara glanced over at them, her husband was gazing down at Arella's tiny face with an expression of enchantment.

Mara didn't yet know if the gauntlet's powers had also touched their child—but for certain, Arella had already put a powerful spell upon her father.

And upon her uncle, too. Soon after Strax and Mara reached the southern shore of the Illwind Sea, they had found Aruk again, and heard all that had befallen him since he'd been swept from their ship. Neither Mara nor Strax had been surprised to meet his pretty bride, Jalisa, or to learn that she was the ruler of Savadon—because from time to time, through the gauntlet's lingering power Mara had seen Aruk and his queen.

For the same reason, Mara had been happy to remain in Savadon during the final month of her pregnancy rather than continue on the road, or to travel with an infant during the heart of winter. Because although she missed her family terribly, Mara had seen them and knew they were well. So she had sent a message ahead, instead, to let them know she would return in the spring.

And when the first flowers bloomed, she and Strax had left for Aremond.

Mara had not expected the fierce clutch upon her heart when they'd crossed the river that served as the kingdom's eastern border. Her family's home was still two days' ride away—yet after risking so much to destroy Solegius, to simply step foot inside Aremond and to know that tyrant king no longer ruled and terrorized the people here…it was *such* a feeling, one she could not describe. Not pride or joy, and yet both of those. Not relief and happiness, and yet both of those. And it seemed as if everything around her was *new*. The old crofters' huts. The plowed earth in the fields. The green hills in the distance. The city gates—and the city itself, too. Buildings now stood with windows unshuttered and doors opened in welcome.

But the people were newest of all. No matter how young or old. They all seemed completely changed, with faces that smiled now, and eyes that looked forward instead of always down, down. Riding through the streets, Mara heard singing that was happy, and laughter that wasn't cruel, and wondered if she had ever truly been here before because the Aremond she knew had been utterly transformed.

In sheer wonder, she studied everything around her—and was aware of how many people were looking back, of all wide-eyed glances aimed in her direction. Or more likely, in Strax's direction. Her fearsome husband always drew stares.

"Mara."

The skin at the back of her neck tightened. Strax only used that very calm, quiet tone when a threat approached. Several times he'd used it on their journey home, when they'd run across bandits and trolls and baleworms— encounters that began with him saying her name in that way, and ended with a slaughter by his sword or by her magic. Now a dozen soldiers rode toward them, hoofbeats rolling like thunder upon the cobblestones, ornate helms gleaming beneath the sun.

The royal guard.

Oh, but she should have expected this. After all, she had killed a king—and had not hidden her face as she'd done it.

Tension coiled through her gut. Perhaps they meant to arrest her, to make her stand trial…*if* whoever ruled Aremond now permitted a trial at all.

But she *had* done what was right. If necessary, she would stand and defend her actions. Not yet, though.

First, she was going home.

Holding Arella securely in one arm, Strax drew his sword with the other and urged his horse closer to hers. "Take the baby, Mara."

Heart pounding, she shook her head. The air around her seemed to sharpen. She heard the cries of wonder and alarm from the people who'd been looking in their direction. Though she didn't glance down at her hands, she knew her skin was glowing—as her eyes were.

She would not harm these men. But she would not let them stop her, either.

"We *are* going home," she told Strax softly.

The soldiers slowed, as if recognizing the danger they suddenly faced. They came to a halt a stone's throw away, the captain of the guard calling out, "Maraserit ik Terin?"

"That is I." Though she was new, too. The Mara who had left this kingdom a year and a half before was not the same Mara who'd returned. "What reason do you seek me out?"

The captain smiled—an expression that seemed of relief and joy, all at once. Then he abruptly dismounted, dropping to one knee and bowing his head. "To escort you to the palace…Your Majesty."

Mara stared at him. Then at the soldiers behind him, who followed suit. Dismounting, kneeling, bowing. Through the streets, spreading through the city, she heard a single echoing cry.

"The queen has finally come! The queen has come home!"

Had everyone gone mad? In disbelief, she looked to Strax. "I cannot be named queen simply because I killed Solegius," she whispered fiercely to him.

Still cradling Arella against his chest, Strax merely shrugged his powerful shoulders and sheathed his sword. "Your people do not seem to agree."

Her people…everyone around them. Because they had been staring at *her*. Not him. Now they cried out her name, cheering and regarding her with so much hope—as if she had done more than use a magical weapon to free them from a tyrant.

A queen should be so much more than that.

Uncertainty shivered through her heart. "I know nothing about how to rule a kingdom."

"And before you entered the tournament, you knew nothing about slaying trolls or climbing giant skulls," he said softly, and the fire of admiration burning in his gaze heated her through. "But you knew that whatever power you wield, you should only use it for what is right and good. So you will be the finest queen who ever sat upon a throne, Mara."

Emotion clogged her throat. Never did Strax's belief in her waver. "And you will be a king."

Again he shrugged. "I have been a king since Wintermere."

Her lips parted in realization. What she had done to gain Aremond's throne was exactly the same as Strax had. "Because you killed Thadus?"

"No, Mara." Taking her hand, he brought it to his mouth and pressed a kiss into her palm, filling her heart with a warmth that smothered the shivering uncertainty. "Because I married you."

Had any woman ever been as blessed as she? For she had a husband who loved her with all of his heart, a beautiful daughter and a wonderful family—and now an entire kingdom believed in her, too.

Yet would Strax be as happy as she was? He had liberated a kingdom with barely any effort. A kingdom he could have ruled—along with many others. Because it had not been the first time he'd freed a realm or killed a king. While in Savadon, she had heard Strax and his brother share tales of the adventures they'd known before the tournament had begun. Surely, even though Strax and Mara were now a king and queen, they could still travel… yet his life would be nothing like what it had been before he'd married her.

So amid all the joy and celebration of that day and of the days that followed, doubt plagued her heart. She could see no discontent in her husband, no restlessness—but perhaps it would come. And if it did…

If it did, then Mara would give up the throne to someone she trusted, and leave with him.

"THAT IS A FACE WISE men would fear."

From her seat in front of the mirror, Mara glanced up to see Strax entering the royal bedchamber from the adjoining nursery. Each recent evening had been finished in this sweet manner—retiring to the queen's quarters after dinner, where Mara would feed the baby and then take her bath while Strax put Arella to bed. Often Mara was already beneath the covers before he reappeared—not because the baby took so long to fall asleep, for she often began slumbering at Mara's breast—but because their days had become so busy and their time together so precious, that Strax would tread the nursery floor with Arella cradled in his arms before finally laying her in the cot.

But this eve, he had not lingered in the nursery very long. Braiding her damp hair, Mara glanced into the mirror. Her skin did not glow and her eyes did not shine.

"*Mine* is a face to fear?"

"It is." Strax crossed the bedchamber toward her, his gaze fixed upon her features. "For that is a face you wear after coming to a decision, and says that only a fool would stand in your way…or you will poison him with the sweetness between your legs."

Mara laughed. "Did I wear such a face that day?"

"You did." He crouched before her chair, and although a smile tilted the corners of his mouth, his dark eyes were solemn when he took her hands in his. "And on that day, your heart ached because you believed that you would have to seek the gauntlet alone. Does it ache now, too? If so, my wife, my queen, tell me what must done to ease your troubles, and I will do it."

So different she was now from that Mara, too. She had never easily shared her worries with anyone—not even her family—and certainly not with Strax in those first months. Yet everything had begun to change between them the first time she had, when she'd confessed that Solegius held her family captive. Then again when she'd told him how his careless words had hurt her for so long. Then again when she had admitted her intention to use the gauntlet. Over the past year, she had gotten better at confiding in him—and although this was a worry she would rather hide, by now she knew it was better to have it out in the open.

With her heart in her throat, she cupped his jaw in her palm. "If ever you become discontented here—if ever you feel caged or trapped—know that I will go with you."

A frown darkened his face. "Caged?"

"Or bored. Or…dissatisfied." Her breath trembled. "You have seen so much of the world and had so many adventures, Strax. And you are not a man who will be happy with only the duties of a king. So if ever you wish to pursue those adventures again, do not hesitate to say so."

His expression lightened and he brought her hand to his mouth, kissed her fingers. "I do not need to pursue adventures."

"That cannot be true. You are—"

"Up to my neck in danger." His teeth nipped at her fingertips. "Did we not receive reports that Solegius's magics had scaled and tainted the forests around Aremond, along with the creatures who live there? Do you think that I would send your armies to die while I am safe within these castle walls—or do you know that I will fight with them?"

"I know you will." As she would, too. "But that is only—"

"Monsters, demons, and slavering beasts. Hardly a challenge," he said, nodding as if in agreement. "Yet there is also the danger your father warned me of—one that I will face all too soon."

Mara sat up straighter. "My father? What danger?"

"A daughter who will soon begin walking." His deep voice was utterly grave. "I have heard how many times I will turn my back for only a moment and find Arella missing. I have heard the terrors every father must face—and that those terrors never lessen, for Arella will grow older, and no longer listen to us, then she might join a tournament and travel away from home, and every moment until she returns will be a torment. And that is only one child. I think we will likely have more, so I'll not have a moment's peace or a chance to become discontented."

Smiling now, Mara said, "Perhaps a few more children."

"Even if we have no more, I would be content to never leave this bedchamber, for the greatest danger I know is here."

So it was. "Because of the magic the gauntlet left in me."

"No. That I do not fear. But with a mere touch of your fingers, Mara…" He pressed her palm over his heart, flattening her hand over steely muscle. "You make me so weak."

Her pulse began to race. "You do not feel weak."

"Do I not?" Gaze molten, he lifted her from the chair and carried her to the bed. "Then we will see if I have strength enough for this adventure. And here is where I will start." Gently laying her atop the covers, Strax came down over her trembling body, his thumb sweeping over her lips. "At the Honeyed Cavern, which might be most dangerous of all."

"How so?" she whispered against his skin.

"Because if from this cavern ever came the words that you do not love me, you would kill me instantly."

An ache slipped down her throat. "Never would I say such words. Always, I will love you."

"Those words kill me, too. But it is the sweetest death, Mara," he said gruffly, before bending his head. "And never will I tire of exploring your Honeyed Cavern."

With kisses, hot and slow—before journeying onward, to her jaw and her neck, where he bestowed more names while tasting and teasing her sensitive skin. Her husband proved to be a poor poet. She shook with laughter as his tongue climbed her Milky Mountains, then gasped in pleasure as he sucked her Rosy Peaks to throbbing points. He stopped to worship at the altar of her belly, then pretended to become lost in the lush forest that guarded the Wondrous Heaven between her thighs.

There he made her come on his tongue, and her shudders of ecstasy were still quaking through her body as he turned her over. He kissed the slopes of her shoulders, explored the shallow valley of her spine—then set her to giggling again when he slipped his fingers along the cleft of her ass, and teased the entrance to her Well of Mystery with the pad of his thumb.

"Perhaps when *you* are feeling more adventurous," he said against her ear—then her giggles dissolved into pure pleasure as he parted her thighs and sank his cock into her wondrous heaven.

This, too, was new. Many times Mara had taken him, yet always she loved him more than the time before. Never had she loved him as much as now. She could not see Strax behind her, but he was all that she could feel—his skin hot and slick, his heavy muscles bunching and releasing, his ragged breaths into her hair.

And he was all that she could feel inside her, too. His steely length filled her sheath, but he was deeper than that. So much deeper. He filled her heart and her thoughts, so there was only him—her husband, leading her to a place that he'd taken her to before, yet never did the journey become old.

Now she pushed back against him, trying to rise onto her knees, crying out with every deep thrust. Driving harder into her sultry heat, he wedged his hand beneath her stomach and his long fingers found her clit—her Magic Pebble, Strax grunted the name as he began to rub, and Mara was laughing again when the orgasm crashed into her, knocking the breath from her lungs, her inner muscles cinching tight as her entire body shook from the force of her release.

His hot seed soon joined the river of need that glistened on her inner thighs, then Strax gathered her close—holding her as he had so many times since she'd become his midnight bride.

Again he kissed her, so sweet and slow, before telling her softly, "Never would I wish for anything other than this, Mara. You *are* everything I could have ever wished for."

Just as Strax was all that she had wished he would be—and so much more. Not a doubt remained as she kissed him, or as she began journeying her way south, licking and tasting.

Because Mara, too, enjoyed an adventure—and her king had a Throbbing Tower to explore.

• END •

S O HERE WE ARE AGAIN, AT THE CLOSE OF A TALE AND DECIDING what more to tell. Did Strax and Mara have more children? Of course they did. Did those children grow up to have adventures of their own? Of course they did. They encountered many obstacles and dangers, had many heartaches and many joys. And they faced them all as their parents had—trusting in the magic of love, but knowing that love is not always enough (and during such times, they usually used a sword).

But those are tales for anotherwhere and anotherwhen. These three tales of brides and their barbarian warriors are finished…apart from answering the most important question at any story's end. Did our heroes and heroines live happily ever after?

Of course they did.

THE
MIDNIGHT
BRIDE
STRAX'S
JOURNEY
Not to scale. Physical features and distances are
exaggerated for clarity and fun.
OCEAN OF NEED
ROSY
PEAK
HONEYED
CAVERN
THE NORTHERN
KISSING TRAIL
MILKY
MOUNTAINS
THE
ALTAR
OF WORSHIP
SEA
OF
DESIRE
LUSH FOREST
WONDROUS
HEAVEN AND
THE MAGIC PEBBLE
KISSING TRAIL
BREEDER
COVE
SEED RIVER
REVERSE VIEW
THE SOUTHERN
WELL
OF
MYSTERY

Author's Note

Hello there, book lovers! I hope you loved reading this collection of novellas! When I first wrote *The Midwinter (Mail-Order) Bride*, I never intended to write a series of stories set in that world, but I had far too much fun to let the Dead Lands go.

Next up is *The Midsummer Bride*! That novel should be available in summer of 2023, and will be coming out with both the original covers in ebook and print, as well as a discreet paperback version to match the others in this series.

And you'll see these characters again! Each of these stories lead into an exciting new series called **Daughters of the Hunt**. I'll have more details soon on my website, and the first book features Kael and Anja's son...along with many other familiar faces from the Dead Lands series.

If you'd like to receive a notification when these books release, please sign up for my newsletter! I promise I'll never spam your or trade your information. I'll only use it to inform you of my new releases.

Until then, happy reading!
Kati

About Kati

Kati Wilde is a tight-lipped, loose-hipped woman of indeterminate age and low breeding. She writes romantic fiction to assuage her darker urge to write Transformers erotica. You can reach Kati by email at kati@katiwilde.com.

Kati Online

Website: katiwilde.com
Twitter: @katiwilde
Instagram: instagram.com/authorkatiwilde
Facebook: facebook.com/authorkatiwilde

www.ingramcontent.com/pod-product-compliance
Lightning Source LLC
Chambersburg PA
CBHW021340150726
47989CB00005B/2049